RED HOUR

AND OTHER STRANGE TALES

PAMELA JEFFS

Published by Four Ink Press 2018
Copyright © 2017 Pamela Jeffs
Extract from 'Birth and Death' © 2017 Maria Williams

Cover design and formatting by BookCoverCafe.com

ISBN:
978-0-6481442-0-5 (pbk)
978-0-6481442-1-2 (e-bk)

Visit www.fourinkpress.com

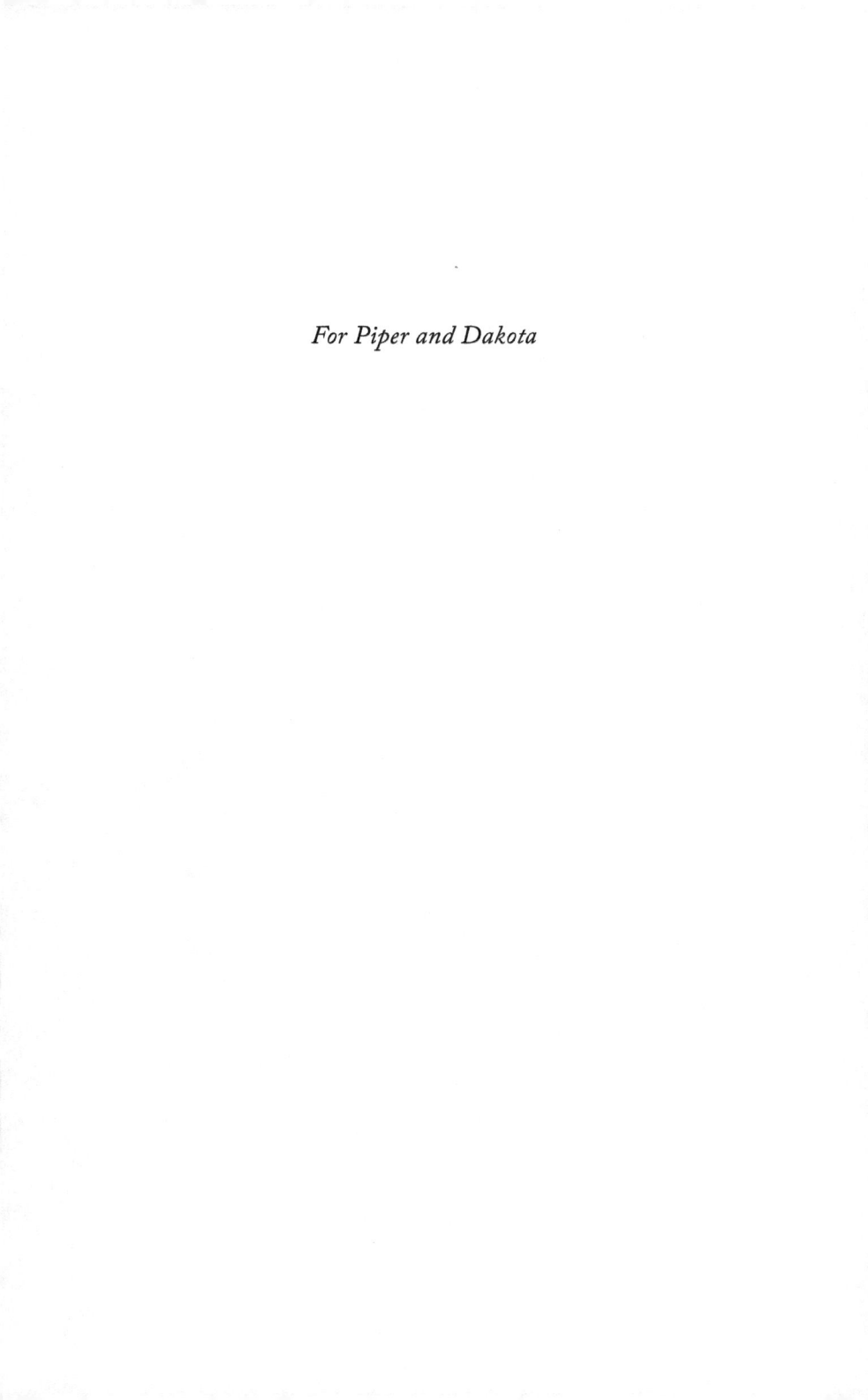

For Piper and Dakota

Contents

Acknowledgments

I would like to acknowledge and thank all the people who have helped this collection come to life.

The editors of the generous organisations and magazines who published the original versions of these stories, and those who have bestowed awards on others.

The Book Cover Cafe team for their guidance and mentorship.

My writing tribe. You know who you are. Thank you for the moral support, the reading of the many drafts, and all the comments and assistance in polishing. You have gone above and beyond, especially when asked to delve into the weird with me. Thank you.

And my mother Maria, for her advice to always start a story with a bang and end with a twist.

But most of all, I would like to thank my husband Darren, and my two daughters, Piper and Dakota. I thank them every day for the time they give me to create, the faith they have in me to succeed, and their unfailing love. If not for them, this book would never have existed.

Thank you all.

Introduction

'Without transformation,
Without a new breath,
Without death would be no life,
Without life, no death.'
— Maria Williams, *Birth and Death*

Transformation is defined as a marked change in form, nature, or appearance.

Australia is a country that embodies this definition. In the space of a single year, one can see calm ocean weather turn savage; wild, dry landscapes shift to soft, flooded plains; bushland blacken by bright fire; and strong people fall victim to all of these various circumstances.

This collection of speculative-fiction stories is inspired by the unpredictable nature of Australia: by her environment and her people. The characters within each story begin in one way and by the end have usually changed mentally, physically or spiritually. Their stories, although fantastical in nature, are a study of the emotional significance of such transformations.

So thank you for investing your time in reading my words. The stories I have crafted are strange, to say the least, but my hope is that there will be something in each one—some emotional connection—that you as a reader can relate to.

Music Box Witch

They have exhausted all legal avenues and are now resorting to violence. Trying to kill a poor woman for refusing to sell her land. Deplorable. But bring it on, I say. Let them try. I will not surrender.

The afternoon shadows wax long as I rush helter skelter through the scrub. I flick aside clutching branches and duck beneath the hanging drapes of orb-weaver webs. In my haste, I barely see the tattered gumtrees or lichen-covered granite boulders. They are just obstacles and I need to get to the clearing.

Caw flies ahead of me. She's a quick black shadow flitting between green branches and ragged patches of copper sky. She is the captain of my Sky Guard and the one who warned me of the assassin.

I was harvesting wild mushrooms in the gully behind my shop when she found me. The man was inside, she'd said. He didn't smell right to her. Evil. But worst of all, the shop girl had just told him where to find me.

I am lucky Caw is so clever. If not for her, I would already be dead.

Behind me, I hear the man curse. He's tripped up on a fallen branch. I hope the thug has broken his ankle.

Caw slices sideways and I follow her lead. She calls out once, her harsh crow cry echoing out through the bush. I can hear her thoughts. Not far now.

I leap over a large fallen tree, startling a flock of jackdaws as I land on the other side. It's my turn to curse as the noisy birds' indignant screeching filters back to the man. I beg them to be silent, but they are not clever birds, jackdaws. They natter at me and pluck at my sleeves as they hop away. The fact that I didn't ask them to join the Sky Guard has obviously not been forgotten nor forgiven.

But their noise is enough to draw attention. I hear the man behind me change course. I start running again. The trees thicken around me.

Caw calls out again. *Here.*

I push my way through the copse of flowering golden wattle she has led me to. The tiny blooms fall around me like a soft, yellow veil. I press harder against the tight-knit branches. They bend and I slip through. The clearing at the heart of the wattle grove finally emerges. This place is called the Hearth. It's where the currents of natural magic in the area run strongest.

The afternoon sun is falling in slanted shards across the clearing, tarnishing the dry grass in tones of rust and copper. Motes of wattle flower hang suspended in the air, the distinctive fragrance strong. Caw waits for me on the edge of the old stone well at the centre of the Hearth. She looks like a black spirit in the fairytale setting.

I sprint the last few steps to the well. I grab the edge, feeling the warmth of the day still held in the stones. I vault up, and with arms held wide I balance myself on the well wall. In the black depths below, I see a glimmer of silver water. The water here is rich with power, and on a better day I would draw it to help cast my spell. But not today. Today, there is no time. Today, I must ask Caw to help me.

I turn around, sucking in air to ease the ragged breath in my throat. I look at Caw and smile. 'Are you ready for this?'

She catches my gaze with one bright eye. Her voice filters into my mind. *Yes, Lily. But what you are about to do is wrong.*

I let my grin fade. 'He's here to kill me, Caw. He deserves what's coming to him.'

She hops two steps away from me and ruffles her long, shining blue-black wings. She settles them back in place. She obviously does not agree.

The cracking sound of breaking branches draws my attention. My gaze swings up to the wattle grove. The sudden, sharp cries of pain from the damaged trees sound out and I feel my anger surge. Why are men never gentle?

The man bursts into the clearing through a curtain of torn leaves and yellow flowers. This is the first clear look I've had of him. He's dressed in tight-fitting black jeans and a hooded jumper. He carries a weapon, a handgun, and sports a dark beard. His lips are peeled back, his teeth clenched in determination. They look so white against his dark hair.

He hasn't seen me yet. But I see him.

I wait, listening to the rasping catch of his breath; smelling the scent of his sweat. Without thinking, I open myself to the unseen spirit currents. Spirit light blooms around me, overlaying the living world. At my left, Caw becomes a bright white star. The wattle trees pulse green with the glow of natural life, red where he has torn the branches away. But the man is revealed as a pillar of darkness.

Caw was right about him.

Evil.

Dark Beard sees me now. He stops running. His voice is rough and hard. 'Get down from there.'

Caw bursts into sudden flight. She spirals upwards into the sky, threads of spirit music trailing from her wingtips. Dark Beard is oblivious as the music rains down around him. His mortal eyes cannot see Caw's power, the power that will awaken the natural world to battle.

In the distance, the wattle trees begin to move. Quietly. Cautiously. They wade toward us through the earth, creeping ever closer.

I smile at Dark Beard. 'I'm not going anywhere.'

He raises his gun. I think he means to shoot me, but he's too late; the trees have reached him. A thin branch whips down and pulls the weapon from his grasp. Dark Beard swears, turning to see what attacked him. Shock creases his features, but he doesn't hesitate. He pulls a short axe free from his side and starts hacking at the trees—sharp, brutal movements that sever branches.

The battle cries of the trees rise in response.

Caw calls out and the earth below responds. It begins to move also, arching and bucking beneath Dark Beard's feet. He cries out as he tumbles sideways. Caw's harsh cry rings out again. Her voice awakens the grass. Long strands burst into life and twist around the man's arms and legs. Soon he is held fast, the axe lying uselessly by his side.

Caw flutters down to rest again on the side of the well. Her music has ended and the trees fall still. The earth shudders into silence. The grass stops twisting, but Dark Beard is still held firm.

It's now safe for me to touch the ground. I jump down from the wall of the well. My booted feet scuff the dry grass as I walk over and stand above Dark Beard. 'You made a mistake following me here.'

He snarls at me; a trapped animal. This close I can see the thin, red veins in his eyes.

'You're the one making the mistake,' he says. 'People like me will just keep coming until you're either dead or decide to sell. The mayor wants this land for the new housing estates and he always gets what he wants.'

'Perhaps,' I reply. 'But then again, he's never tangled with a music-box witch before.'

A puzzled look crosses the man's face. 'A what?'

'Let me show you.'

I open my hand. A small wattle flower floats down from one of the trees and settles in my palm. I whistle a low note. The flower turns to light and floats upwards. Next, a small stone rises from the ground and also settles in my palm. It's followed by a green leaf, a drop of water from the well, a blade of dry grass.

5

Caw sidles over. I know she doesn't want to do this, but she doesn't want me dead either. She shakes her head and a tiny black feather falls to join the other items in my hand.

I whistle again to activate the spirit music that resides in each element. Soon a gathering of tiny multi-coloured lights floats in front of me, each a powerful note of spirit music. I shuffle the notes about. Soon they're assembled into a melody of light, colour and warmth.

I glance back at Dark Beard. 'I'm sorry, but this may hurt a little.'

I don't wait for his reply. I gather the strand of music and send it towards his darkness. It enters easily. He screams.

I do not delight in his pain. But this small stretch of Australian bushland does not have the force of a raging ocean or the might of a volcano to defend it. It has only me, a lowly music-box witch.

I watch as lines of coloured light start to mix with the blackness of Dark Beard's being. It's like watching oil mix with vinegar. His screams grow louder as not only his essence is changed, but his physical form also.

Caw shifts uncomfortably at my side. I can feel her disapproval like heat from an open forge. But she is young. She does not understand. She has never been caged nor seen an entire forest torn free of the earth that birthed it. I have, and I refuse to let it happen again.

Dark Beard is almost consumed now by my spirit music. He is a tower of spinning light, seething and glittering in the dusk. His screams fade and the gyrating tower begins to reduce down in size until it's a single, incandescent spirit-light star resting on the grass.

I shift my awareness back to the real world. The star fades. In its place rests a small, polished mahogany box. I reach down and open the lid. A tiny, carved stone figure begins to rotate on a spindle. It's Dark Beard, and he's dancing to the melody I made from a flower, a stone, water, grass and the feather of a magic bright-eyed crow.

As I watch him spinning I wonder how the mayor will look, dancing in one of my boxes.

I, Mutineer

The water laps outside the hull. The gentle slap of salty brine is a lullaby to remind me of other days; days when I could feel a kind breeze on my brow, and sunlight on my skin; days before I was chained to an oar bench in the dark hold of Davy Jones's phantom ship.

Light does not penetrate here except for a thin beam filtering in through a section of broken caulking. It does not break the darkness of the hold, but instead marks a bright day outside, one I will never see. Around me, that same darkness hides the features of my fellow prisoners, but their heaving breaths rumble on, a soft roar of sound that is both quiet and loud. These people pull at the oars as I do. This is the punishment given to first mates that mutiny against their captains—and fail, just as I did.

I may not be able to see their faces, but I can recognise some of my fellow prisoners by the scent of their sweat. The man to my left smells like onions, the one to my right like salt. I can only imagine what I smell like, and it won't be the scent of gardenia I once favoured. In this place we are never permitted to talk, so I don't know the true names of Onion and Salt, but I have hauled oars by their side for years now, making these men as close to me as brothers.

I try to avoid it, but always my thoughts turn to my old captain, Tyrell. A bastard of a blackbirding pirate, cruel to his men and crueller to the human cargo he hauled illegally through the straits. I remember the day he made me walk the plank, the first woman ever to do so aboard his ship. I still feel the weight of the cannonball he tied to my ankles, the pressure of his cutlass against the small of my back ...

That day had been bright, an azure arc of sky reaching down to touch the horizon at both sides of the world. The sea, as I remember it, was a sparkling swatch of blue cloth rippling into the distance, the sun a fierce golden sphere above us. But the kindness of the day was not felt upon Captain Tyrell's vessel, the *Revenge*.

The deck was a mess of scarlet, with a pile of black-skinned bodies stacked against the mast. The bloodstained deck boards were slippery, a treacherous hazard for footing already made uneven by the rolling swell of the ocean.

As first mate, I had been permitted to stand clear of the chaos. At the wheel, I watched the events unfold below.

A woman was dragged up from the hold, her fine ebony skin glowing like black metal in the sunlight. Despite her incarceration, her dark eyes were full of fire. I recognised her. I'd seen her fighting on the beach the day she was captured. She was the warrior woman with twin spears flashing, slicing, cutting ... She is the tribal elder's daughter.

As she was led past the mast, her eyes fell on the corpse of her father, stacked there with the other warriors who had broken free and led the below-deck attack the previous night. I saw grief flare in her eyes, saw the tiny stumble of her feet. But beyond that she showed nothing. So proud and so fierce were those slaves Tyrell had taken from the wild coast of Australia.

Tyrell, with long blond beard and wide-brimmed hat, stood formidable upon the deck. His red mongrel dog sat loyal by his side, red tongue lolling. Tyrell seemed un-cowed by the glare the woman fixed on him. Instead, he smiled at her, white teeth glinting. And then, in mock salute to her status, he raised the bloodied cutlass hanging from his bloodied hand

'Kneel,' he said, but even I could see she would do no such thing.

'You kneel before *me*, pirate,' she'd replied.

The men had laughed. Tyrell's face had darkened. And I'd found myself unexpectedly inspired by the woman's outright defiance of a man I inherently feared. Suddenly, I didn't want to see her lying dead like her father.

I gestured to the cabin boy standing by my side. 'Hold the ship steady.'

He looked frightened as he grasped the wheel.

I headed for the lower deck, my hand held lightly to my small sword.

I watched as Tyrell gestured to the boatswain. The large man, a powerhouse of muscle, stepped forward and dragged the woman to her knees. She fought him. She fell hard. I saw her features twist with pain.

I pulled my sword free. I lunged at Tyrell. His dog barked.

He moved.

I missed.

And now here I am; not even knowing the final outcome of the woman I tried to save.

I steady my rapid breathing. If I ruminate on the injustice of my fate, my despair gets the better of me. Last time, I'd started screaming. The ghouls that guard us saw me removed from my chains, whipped, and strapped to the mast for a full season; a season that had felt like eternity.

Or perhaps it *had* been eternity. I have no way of knowing for sure.

Days, hours and minutes—time works differently aboard this ship.

I feel a hand reach over and squeeze my wrist. It's Onion. His gesture conveys his message. *Settle yourself, darlin'. Not worth going up again.*

He's right. But something has to give.

My mind churns. I am a mutineer surrounded by mutineers; if united, surely we could fight our way off this cursed ship.

It's not like we have anything to lose.

It's not like we can die again.

I readjust my grip on the oar. Yes, it's time: time to make a plan.

Time to change my fate.

Spirit of the Earth

The air, like the earth, was dry. Thirsty. I dropped my shovel and walked back to the patch of shade that lingered beneath the spindly limbs of John's gumtree. I sat down on the rock that I had positioned next to his gravestone, picked up my saddle pack and dug about until I found my water flask. I unscrewed the top and held the flask to my parched lips.

The water was warm and tasted slightly salty. Bore water always tasted like that. John told me it was the mineral salts leaching from the ground that did it. He had been clever in knowing about things like that. Maybe it was because, unlike me, he had grown up in a big, faraway city, gone to school and learned to read.

I grew up with only my father on the station. For the last twenty years, he had taught me to read landscapes, weather patterns and animal tracks, but there was never much time for written texts.

'It's bloody hot out in that sun, John. You'd better like this garden when I'm done.'

I glanced at his gravestone. Dappled patterns of sunlight filtered down through the leaves above and danced across the pale pink sandstone block. The outline of the image I had carved on it stood out in sharp relief. It wasn't an exact likeness of his profile, but it was the best I could do. I knew he wouldn't mind. He always told me he liked my drawings of him even when they hadn't been perfect.

I sighed. I wished John were still here. I missed our conversations.

A hot breeze fanned its way across the dry creek bed, bringing with it the sound of cicada song. I felt the sweat on my skin dry, making it feel taut. The same breeze made Gus, my horse, snort from his place by the tree. With his nose cleared, he shifted his weight onto his other leg, tilting a back hoof in idle repose as he resettled.

A small whirly-whirly kicked up suddenly in the sun-drenched basin of the creek. It skipped and danced across the cracked clay, spinning a handful of dried leaves and grass upwards as it went. I smiled, watching as it tracked crazy patterns across the earth.

My father would say that the whirly-whirly meant that evil spirits were close by. He was superstitious when it came to the old aboriginal legends. But not me; I saw beauty in the whirly-whirly, beauty in the landscape that it belonged to. That's why I chose this place by the creek for John. It was where I would like to be buried when my time came.

Still, I could hear John's voice in my head, questioning. *It's a lovely place you picked for me, Jane, but why the garden?* I could just see him, cocking his tousled blond head and rolling those laughing green eyes of his at me.

I smiled wider at the thought, my bottom lip cracking as I did so. I licked thoughtfully at the blood that beaded to the surface, and then I chuckled out loud. I was certain he would have thought me crazy.

But then again, John hadn't been one to value the importance of little things the way I did. Perhaps being an RAAF pilot and having witnessed the true scale of the world meant his eye had only ever been drawn to the extraordinary. It wasn't surprising, coming as he had from the modern part of this 1930s world; a part filled with the likes of airplanes, ever-expanding cities and manmade gardens.

My world was one of cattle, red earth and blue sky. I had never seen any of those other things, especially gardens like he had described. He had often spoken of his mother's garden in Darwin and how it had been the only place that had ever felt like home.

'A green place of solemn beauty,' he had called it.

Here, in my land of red dust, silver bark and dusty green trees, I think he missed that garden most of all. When he knew he was dying, I think he would have liked to see it one last time. But it was not to be. The injuries from the plane crash that saw him stranded here with us were more than I had the skill to heal. In our short time together we had become friends. In fact, he was the first real friend I had ever had. Building this garden for him was my way of saying both thank you and goodbye.

I glanced down at the few wilted plants that I had carefully gathered for the job: wattle saplings, Sturt's desert peas, and a trailing vine of jasmine that I had pilfered from behind the cattle yards. The plants sat waiting; their roots bundled in dampened strips of canvas. I sighed. They seemed a far cry from the flowers

John had described, but to me they were the very best the drought-stricken heart of Australia had to offer.

I screwed the lid of the water flask back into place and put it on the ground next to my sitting rock. 'Back to work,' I said.

I got to my feet and readjusted the brim of my hat. I reached down and picked up the box of small plants that awaited their new home. They seemed so fragile, but I knew there was moisture in the ground near the creek, even if the water didn't flow along the top anymore. Hopefully it would be enough to see them flourish.

I walked over, kneeled down next to the shovel and set the box to one side. I dug my fingers into the red earth. It was dry and powdery at the top, but felt damp below. I unwrapped the delicate roots of each plant and placed them into the holes I had made. It didn't take long to settle them in and press the soft earth back firmly over their bases. I sat back on my heels and looked at my work. They were a motley array of plants, but I thought them beautiful.

I dusted my hands clean and got to my feet. I went to grab the shovel, but something made me pause.

I looked out across the dried creek bed to the scattered trees and yellow Mitchell grass that lined the opposite bank. Something felt different. My shovel had not moved, the whirly-whirly still danced, and the cicadas still chirruped, but there was a sense of expectancy in the air, a stillness that existed without the absence of sound.

Then the whirly-whirly subsided.

A twig snapped behind me.

I turned so quickly that a cloud of red dust dislodged itself from the brim of my hat. My gaze fell upon the sitting rock.

It was no longer empty.

A tiny man, if you could call him that, was crouching on the rock. Beneath the kangaroo-fur smock he wore, his skin shone silver and was scaled like a lizard's. Wide, dark eyes stared at me from beneath a bedraggled mop of blue-black hair. His nose wrinkled as he sniffed at me, and I noticed a scattering of ochre-and-white dots painted across the bridge of it. The pattern reminded me of the boomerang my father had hanging in the living room at home.

'What are you doing?' His voice was husky, sounding like the whisper of wind over stone.

'Building a garden,' I replied, too shocked to do anything but answer.

The little man leaned over to look at my work. He raised an eyebrow. 'This is a garden?'

I glanced back at the plants and suddenly felt embarrassed. Before, I had thought how beautiful they looked, but I now saw them for what they were: a pathetic row of seedlings that probably wouldn't survive.

I turned back and squared my shoulders, ignoring the little man's sarcastic grin. 'I don't need your approval. Go away.'

The little man jumped off the rock, his bare feet landing in a cloud of dust. He sauntered up to the plants with his hands locked together behind his back. He bent at the waist and sniffed at them. He shook his head and swivelled his eyes up to meet mine. 'These do not belong here,' he said.

I felt my anger rising.

'No, not at all,' he continued. 'The wind chose elsewhere for them to grow. Take them back to their place.'

'This land belongs to me. I will do what I want with it.'

The little man's eyes glittered like chips of black mirror. 'Land does not belong to one,' he said, 'one belongs to *it*.'

I was done listening. I bent over, picked up the shovel and leaned it across my shoulder. 'The garden stays,' I said. 'I'll be back to check on it. I wouldn't do anything to try and ruin it, if I were you.' I turned away, heading towards Gus.

'Wait,' called out the little man after me. 'I'll help make it better.'

I stopped and turned. I wanted the best for John. 'What did you have in mind?'

The little man smiled an evil little grin. 'A dreaming flower.'

'A what?'

The little man pulled his hand out from behind his back. A shiny red seed lay nestled in the tiny cradle of his palm. 'A flower to hold memory,' he said. 'Put your memories into the seed, plant it and it grows. Memories make the colour; each flower is unique. It's bush magic.'

Bush magic? I didn't trust him, but there was something compelling about the seed. It glittered so brightly in his palm, as if it was transparent and the sun itself shone out from its ruby heart.

I was suddenly kneeling in the dirt, reaching out for the seed. Just as my fingers made to close over it, the little man snatched it back to his chest. I stifled a cry of dismay.

He smiled again. 'Plant it by your friend's grave.'

He was right. I nodded and got back to my feet. I walked out of the broad sunlight and again entered the shade. I sat down on the sitting rock.

'Now put your memories in,' the little man said, nodding encouragingly. He dropped the seed into my hand.

17

The seed felt hot against my skin. Searing, almost. I wrapped my fingers around it and closed my eyes, thinking of John. I put his kind smile into the seed, and my enjoyment of the worldly conversations we had shared on the old veranda. There were the heartfelt compliments of my drawing skills, and the memory of how his eyes crinkled when he laughed at my jokes. I steered away from the memories of his last few days, the smell of his gangrenous leg, the grey tinge to his skin, and the helplessness of knowing that real doctors were too far away to help him.

Suddenly I felt the seed move in my hand. It twitched with life and then, to my horror, I felt it burrow into my skin. I opened my hand, but the seed was gone. There was no blood, but I could feel it moving through my hand and up my arm towards my heart.

'What's happening?' I screamed at the little man.

He just stood there, his face grim. 'I am a spirit of the earth, I belong to this land,' he said, 'And now, so will you.'

I tried to reply, but my tongue was tied. My limbs jerked outward as a searing pain tore through my body. In horror, I watched my fingers change. Each one became a petal: dark blue spotted with white.

My palms turned bright orange and filled with pollen, each becoming the heart of a flower. A glistening red seed burgeoned suddenly into existence, cocooned in the core of each one.

My body lengthened and my feet dug into the ground. My toes became roots, and I felt them burrow deeper and deeper into the earth. With them, I tasted moisture; I tasted mineral salt; I tasted the dead timber of John's coffin.

Before my eyesight failed, I saw myself reflected in the dark orbs of the little man's eyes. I had become a flowering tree. Unique. Striking. I tried to cry out, but no sound came. My hearing was the last of my senses to fade, the final sound I heard that of the little man's voice.

'Beautiful,' he whispered, as I felt him pluck the red seeds from my palms.

Red Hour

Sunset. Red hour. And it arrives heralded by a dark, riderless horse. Its eyes are wild, its hooves thundering as it emerges from a cloud of red dust. For a moment I think Chris, my off-sider, has returned from his hunt for water. But no, there is no rider, just the unknown horse. It's a bad omen.

I stand up, the fire I'm tending forgotten. The small cluster of cattle we've spent the day herding scatters as the frantic horse, loose stirrups flying, barrels into camp. Clumps of broken earth fly free from the animal's hooves. It's only with luck that I manage to catch hold of a streaming rein. I plant my feet firmly. The horse pulls around to an uneasy stop.

The animal is a stallion, muscled and tall. I grab his bridle. His eyes roll, showing a sickening glare of white.

'Whoa, boy,' I croon to him.

But the horse is afraid. I see it in the stretch of his neck and hear it in the race of his breath. This horse wants to keep running. I try to calm him by trailing my fingertips down his dusty neck.

He shies violently from my touch. But I hold him firm. He settles into uneasy submission.

From under the brim of my hat, I let my gaze travel along his neck and over his shoulder. The poet in me sees the beauty in his terror: in the strained lines of his tendons and in the velvet flare of his nostrils. There is music even in the saddle he wears; the black leather scratched and dented. But now is not the time for poetry.

The saddle sits high against the horse's wither. The hide above it is matted, the hair threaded through with an unsettling stain of colour: dark red against russet desert dust. I touch it. My fingers come away sticky. Blood. But there's no injury to the animal. Perhaps it belongs to a rider lost. I curse. A rider I'll now have to go out alone to try and find.

I turn to lead the stallion around to the picket line where the other horses are tethered, but the animal refuses. He rears, breaking free of my grip on the reins. I can do nothing but watch as he gallops away into the bleeding dusk.

Outlined by the sunset's light, the stray horse's tracks are easy to follow. I backtrack down the line of prints, to where he came from rather than where he went. My own mount, Billie, glad to be free of her tether, trots easily through the sparse red landscape; a landscape dotted here and there with low stretches of saltbush and the odd twisted gum.

As we top a low rise, the tracks of the dark horse become muddled. Hoof prints pressed into torn earth become tangled with a scattering of boot prints. Strange. Did the rider fall here before the horse bolted?

I look out toward the horizon, squinting against the brightness of it. There are no clear answers. I lower my gaze to follow the tracks that fall away down the side of the rise. They end at a nearby cluster of wattle trees. Perhaps the answers will be there.

There is a clearing at the centre of the wattle grove, a circular carpet of long yellow grass that begins and ends at the boundary of the trees. The trees themselves are, on closer inspection, bizarre. I have never known wattle trees to bleed red sap.

Billie won't enter the clearing. I leave her at the edge, the reins tied to a leaking wattle branch. The strange sap has her sidling away from the tree, and trembling when her hindquarters brush against another.

I never dismiss the caution of animals. I pull my shotgun free from the saddle holster.

At the centre of the clearing, there is a single, twisted stump visible through the grass. Its gnarled top is slightly wedge shaped, reminding me of a granite boulder weathered by rain and wind. And around it, something is staining the grass to rust.

The hair on my neck rises. Hesitantly, I approach, my gun held tightly in my grip.

The razor-edged grass whispers against my legs as I walk. *Shush. Shush.* I pass by a bloodstained linen shirt, crumpled and discarded, a set of cracked leather boots lying on their side, riding chaps, a man's ring glinting gold against the golden grass: all possessions seeming too important to be so casually tossed aside.

Something is wrong about this place. I feel it in my bones. Every fibre in me is screaming, *Run.*

The stump.

It's not a stump at all. It's a timber carving of a naked man, head down and arms clutched around his knees. The detail is astonishing; thin, delicate lines of hair and fingernails are etched in silver against the weathered grey timber. The shoulders of the sculpture are broad, the skin thick and grooved like the bark on an ironbark tree. I would consider it a work of art except for the fact that it sits in a patch of grass that is leaking blood.

Blood.

And ants are crawling everywhere. Their minute industry carries them over the carved shoulders of the sculpture; they carry on their backs droplets of blood harvested from the grass. A centipede treks its way across the gnarled forearm of the man.

The carving is so lifelike I almost expect it to move and brush the insects away.

Then it does move.

I see the carved shoulders rise and the weathered chest expand as the man takes in a deep shuddering breath. And the breath conveys the depths of a great pain.

I drop the gun to the ground and kneel by the strange man. I place my hands, palm down, on the grass to try and get a better look at his face. I snatch them away quickly. Red welts mark my skin; the grass has sliced open my palms. I suddenly have the unsettling feeling that the grass is not leaking blood at all, but instead has an appetite for it.

I shudder and brush my palms down my shirt. The pain fades.

I glance back at the man. 'Are you okay?' It's a stupid question, but the first that comes to mind.

The man shifts, and his arms fall away from his knees. Hair hangs down across his forehead, concealing his eyes. But I can see his lips. They move. His voice, thick and ponderous like sap in a tree, is a whisper.

'I found a riderless horse,
It led me to the copse,
It laid me out on carnivorous grass,
My fate soon will come to pass.
And like the others who here weep,
Amongst the wattle I will sleep.'

The words crawl up my spine. I recognise the power in the poetry. There is truth behind the words and the rhythm.

The fleeing stallion: *a riderless horse.*

Grass drinking blood: *carnivorous grass.*

Trees weeping red sap: *like the others who here weep.*

My blood runs cold. I need to get out of here. I reach out and grab the man's hand. It's then that I realise that he is warm-blooded and not made of timber at all. It's his skin. It's lacking blood; the grass he is sitting on is bleeding him dry of life and colour.

I get to my feet and try to heave the man upright. He weighs heavy, like a piece of timber, and I stumble.

'It's too late, April,' he whispers. 'Leave me and go. And for fuck's sake, don't ride any black horses you find.'

His words turn my stomach to ice. I know this man. He is no stranger.

This man is Chris.

24

The world tilts around me on its axis. Suddenly, I find strength I never knew I had. I haul Chris upright, ignoring his sharp intake of breath.

He seems to realise I don't intend to leave him. He rallies, leaning hard against me as I half drag him toward the perimeter of trees. A line of bloodied grass follows our passage, the plants taking what sustenance they can from Chris's naked legs.

The trees seem to clutch at us as we break past the inner perimeter. The sigh of the wind in their branches sounds even more like the weeping of women and children. I sob, my fear threatening to undo me.

Next to me, Chris stumbles. 'Get up!' I scream, but he is done. I grab him from beneath his arms and drag him the last few feet.

Finally, we clear the trees. I lay Chris gently on the good, clean desert earth.

His dark eyes are open, taking in the final blushed hues of the sunset overhead: pink, purple and azure. 'Thank you,' he whispers, his voice a sigh against his lips. 'I'm sorry, April.'

'Shhh. This isn't your fault.'

'My horse ... broke his leg ... had to shoot him.' Chris's silver, grey fingers worry at the earth beneath them. 'The black horse found me. Tried to ride him back, but the devil brought me here ...' Chris sighs, a single deep exhalation that seems to carry the weight of infinite regret.

Then his fingers stop moving. His eyes lose focus. And he is gone.

My mouth goes dry. I reach down to close his eyes, but the moment is stolen from me as his body begins to sink into the earth and is consumed. A thin green sapling burgeons to life in his place. I scuttle backwards as the seedling grows quickly into a tree.

A wattle tree.

A wattle tree weeping red sap.

And like the others who here weep, amongst the wattle I will sleep.

The poet in me sees the beauty of Chris's end, but the Jillaroo reels with shock. The dichotomy of my emotions renders me still. I sit for long moments, staring at the plant through a blurring of tears.

Death becomes life, becomes death.

There is nothing further I can do here. I get to my feet, brushing away my tears. I look about for Billie. Only now do I realise she's gone. Frantic, I hunt for her tracks, but it's hard to see anything in the fading light.

My gaze scans the horizon, and I'm hoping against hope she is still close by. I see the low rise I rode down earlier and my breath catches in my throat. On the crest, against the canvas of the dying red hour, stands a riderless horse, watching me.

It's the black stallion.

And all I know is, I will not be riding him for anything.

Greysin's March

The coarse volcanic ash caught in the wisped snarls of Greysin's dreadlocks and in the back of his throat. He coughed, but it didn't help. It never helped. Ever since the eruption, the air had been tainted. Greysin reached back for his threadbare scarf. Twisting it, he secured the scrap over his nose and mouth. He lowered his chin and resumed his march through the dead city.

Ash-coated facades of abandoned buildings filed by him like pale ghosts. He felt as if the empty windows stamped into the walls were watching him. In some ways he wished they were. It would mean another sign of life.

But Greysin knew he was alone.

For days after it happened, he had searched the city but found no other survivors. He only kept going, kept searching, because it was either that or die, and he wasn't ready to give up. So he walked on, watching the ground and counting out each footstep as it was etched into the inches of ash that covered everything.

He let all else pass by in a blur. The charred trees that lined the roadways, the dead cars crumpled against shattered gutters and the ash-covered corpses of citizens still sitting within them. Sometimes he thought he could hear the people calling to him, begging, pleading. Or perhaps it was his own ghosts that haunted him. He wasn't certain anymore.

Greysin halted. He lifted his head. He could hear the music again: his daughter's violin. The sound was coming from ahead. But he could see nothing through the curtain of falling ash. He rubbed his eyes, dislodging ash from his eyelashes. Still nothing.

He stopped himself from breaking into a run. He had been disappointed so many times before. But he was definitely hearing music; what if he wasn't going mad like he thought? What if this time it was real?

The song was faint, a thin melody. Greysin heard silent words floating in each note. He heard his daughter calling to him in the cadence of the tune, felt the strains of her music push past the boundaries of his grief and instil within him hope.

'Daddy?' Her voice was barely a sigh against the silence of the city.

'I'm coming, sweetheart,' he whispered, the words cracking over his tongue.

The music faded briefly, but then surged, louder. Greysin broke into a tired run. She was waiting. He must find her. Would the others be with her?

An intersection materialised from the ash and volcanic darkness. The music stopped. The crossroad was empty, no footprint marring the ashy surface. Just like every other time he had followed the music, there was no one waiting for him.

Greysin glanced up at the streetlights that stood like sentinels at each junction. North. South, east and west. Four lights. Four compass points, one for each of the lives lost because his strength had failed him: his wife, his two sons and his daughter.

Greysin squeezed his eyes closed, trying to shut out the memories. Their screams as they had slipped from his hands, swallowed by the mudslide; the feral desperation he had felt as he dug barehanded through the slop in a futile effort to save them.

Greysin opened his eyes. He looked down at his trembling hands. They were broad, and seemed as though they should be strong, but he knew looks were deceiving. He hunched his shoulders and pulled his worn jacket closer. Once again ghosts had led him astray.

He stepped out onto the roadway; ash shifted in eddies around his calves. He looked left and then right. Which way to go? Where could the people be? Left, he decided. He clenched his jaw. He walked on.

He almost missed the sound from behind him. It was a whisper against the profound silence that held the city. It had been so long since he had heard a real sound that it almost seemed unreal. He twisted on his heel, falling into a wary crouch. His fingers clutched at the service revolver he kept concealed at his side, the one he had carried when being a police officer mattered. He pulled it free.

A black dog stood silently in the middle of the road. Its lolling tongue was a shock of red against the impossible white of its teeth. Its eyes were pale blue. Greysin shuddered; his own eyes were that colour. Greysin waited. The dog seemed to be waiting also.

The animal was thin and starving, but Greysin saw in its bearing the mark of a survivor. Even worn so thin, the dog was no victim to its circumstance. Its life spark was vital, bright; the dog, if Greysin dared to believe it, was real.

A sudden desperation gripped him. He holstered the gun and reached into his pocket for his last precious scrap of dried meat. He held it out. The dog extended its nose and sniffed, testing the scent of Greysin's offering on the air. One step followed another as the animal approached with caution. Greysin drank in the details: the coarseness of its fur, the sprinkling of white across its muzzle, the gold tag that hung from the faded red leather collar circling its neck.

The dog stopped a few steps away. It stretched out its neck, lips extended to snatch at the meat. The dog's teeth caught at Greysin's fingers and he almost laughed aloud in delight. Such close contact with another living creature was intoxicating.

With the meat secured, the dog skittered away. A snap of its jaws and the morsel was gone. The dog twisted to look back at Greysin, its long thin tail wrapped like a whip around its rear legs. *Any more?*

'No more,' whispered Greysin.

The dog stood up straight, ears pointed forward. It walked up to Greysin, eyes imploring.

'I'm sorry. No more.'

The dog seemed to understand. It looked up the street in the direction that Greysin had been heading. It pushed its head into Greysin's hand. *Let's go.*

Greysin reached down, lifted the dog's nametag and thumbed away the ash coating it. The writing beneath was scratched, but he could make it out. 'Your name is Delusion?'

The dog's eyes glowed as they held Greysin's gaze.

Greysin smiled. He let go of the collar and began to walk up the road. Around him the city was dead. Its people were dead. The land was dead. But at least he had the dog by his side. Greysin kept walking, choosing to ignore the fact that the animal left no footprints in the ash as it passed.

The Fallen

The breeze raises dust from the dirt road. There's no haste in the motion, only a slow red bloom of particles that curls up and hangs for an instant before falling back and settling into place. It's the only movement in a sparse desert landscape made up of red dirt and the scattered skeletons of long-dead trees.

Other than the sound of the wind, and the ocean booming away against the far coast, the world is silent. No humans, no animals, no life. Nothing sentient except me.

It's midday and the sun is blistering overhead. My mouth is dry. I reach for my oil bottle, the liquid inside sloshing as I tip it up to drink. Only two mouthfuls before it empties. Time to head back home for more. I return the bottle and press the button on my wrist.

Engage.

A click and a whir, and my mechanical wings extend. Their metal length gleams in the midday heat. I kick off from the dead earth and am airborne.

The wind whines and shrieks past my ears. I tip my left aileron and wheel toward the coast. The water sparkles in the distance. Ingrained habit has me searching the ground as I go. I've been doing this for a hundred long years. Searching. I don't really expect to find anyone anymore, but my programming maintains my drive.

Seek out humanity. Search and salvage.

And so I, Ena Unit, prototype robotic search-and-rescue android, search. It was the purpose given to me by the scientists at the Institute of Life for Humanity. I was the only android they had the parts to perfect; I was their only hope. Find and rescue any humans who survived the final world war. That was my duty.

But I was doomed to failure. Those scientists, they sent me out too late. The chemical wars had already torn the world apart by the time I arrived. All that was left were the toxins—toxins that eventually killed every living thing.

The last living human had been my mother, for want of a name, she who designed and activated me. She was Athena Panos, an industrial designer. Her last words still ring in my ears.

'You are alpha and omega, Ena,' she said, 'the beginning and the end. Take what's left of the world and make it yours.'

I often think of when she died; the feeling of her aged fingers slipping free of my wrist; the faraway look that manifested in her eyes. I buried her in the fashion of her people: deep in the ground, cradled by warm earth. It was what she would have wanted, I think.

After that, I left the facility. I couldn't bear to stay. The silence within its concrete walls was overwhelming.

My thoughts are drowned out as my eye catches a glint of light below me: a flash of white against the red desert. Mechanical debris. I tilt my wings and descend.

Working parts are now the only things I search for. And here I've found a fallen drone. Half buried in the sand, the circular machine is battered and yet it holds promise. Its eight rotor blades are rusted to nondescript lumps of ore, but the outline of letters marked on the weathered plastic casing can still be seen: *DAx25*.

I search my data banks. The information is easy to find. It's a cloud-seeding drone, and was manufactured in the year 2200 for the purpose of helping to increase rainfall over desert areas.

I run my fingers across her curved lines. 'Hello, pretty lady,' I whisper.

I lever my fingers in beneath the edge of the drone's carcass and pull it free. A curtain of dirt and rocks cascades over my boots. The grit rises in a blinding cloud, interrupting my vision sensors for a moment. They soon clear. The drone is free of her grave.

She is a metre in diameter. Not large and not heavy, which is a good thing. I turn her over. The twisted mess of rusted wiring and plastic looks to be impossible, but I can see past all that. There is only one part I'm interested in and there's a good chance it's still intact.

I grip the drone with both hands and resume my flight. I no longer scan the ground as I fly, but head straight for the coast.

* * *

It's loud inside my sea cave. The crash of waves as they pound the shore below the cliffs reverberates like thunder off the salt-slick stone. I know salt is not good for working machinery, but I can't help but be drawn to this place. I like the sound of it. The roar and boom. It drowns out the silence of the world, and in hearing it, I don't feel so lonely.

I gently lay out the drone on my workbench. I tease at the seam in the casing. The weatherworn plastic cracks apart like an eggshell to reveal the inner workings. A nested tumble of seized wiring and plastic components stares back at me. My metal fingers have no problem digging through them to the core of the machine. Rust and dirt trickles past my touch and onto my bench.

Then I find it. The component: small, smooth, still intact. My heart gears begin to whir faster. I curl my fingers around the spherical part and pull it free: the drone's brain-core module.

There's something strange about the metal casing. The stainless steel is pitted with corrosion. The marks are unlike anything I've ever seen. They are green, and track unevenly along the surface of the module like human veins. And my thermal sensors detect warmth in the metal. Not warmth that has come by the sun, but the warmth I remember as belonging to the living, to the humans.

I trace my finger along the marks. The metal is impregnated with corrosion. Perhaps years of contact with the chemicals in the earth have changed it somehow.

I turn and rummage through the oilcans that line the shelf behind my bench. The first two are empty, but the third rewards me with the satisfying glugging sound of clean oil swilling in the bottom. I pull out a dented bathing tray and pour in the oil. I hold back from emptying the can and take only a mouthful. I lift the can and swallow. I relish the thick liquid as it trickles down my throat, coating and cleaning away from my gears the dust collected from the day.

I place the empty oilcan on the bench and lift the drone's module. It slips silently out of my fingers and into the bowl. I imagine I can hear a sigh from the component as the soothing bath soaks and loosens frozen data chips. I smile. It's been a long time since I've had access to enough oil to have an immersive bath. But my memory of it is treasured.

I turn toward the pallet that's laid out next to the bench. The long board is supported by the rugged bulk of two water-worn boulders.

On it, a human-shaped figure lies covered with a salt-rimed canvas cover.

The cover falls away stiffly. The glint of well-oiled metal follows. Long, supple legs, and arms ending in fine fingers lie lax against the weathered pallet board. Two long silver wings are neatly folded at each side of the mechanical body. A face made of smooth, copper-coloured metal faces the ceiling. The moulded eyes are closed.

I reach over and unhinge the face. It falls to the left and hangs like a type of grotesque metal mask. Inside, the wiring and an empty brain-core module cradle are exposed. After a century in my care, the parts still look new.

I turn back to the oil bath and pull the drone's component clear. Oil, now tarnished green, drips through my fingers and onto the stone floor. I use a rag to wipe away the excess.

I hesitate as I hold the module over the open cradle. This moment feels frozen. I've waited so long for the chance to activate the sister android I salvaged from the facility: Thea Unit. With her by my side, I will no longer be alone on this dead planet. I have dreamt of our conversations, of the endless days we will spend gliding together through empty, sunlit skies.

I lean over. The module clicks into place.

I close the faceplate.

I wait.

The first sign of activation is the flexing of her metal fingers. Then a mechanical sigh whispers out over polished metal lips.

My heart gears quicken.

Her eyes open.

Something is wrong.

Thea's eyes aren't the typical plastic lenses of an android. They are human. Green. Moist. Alive.

I stumble backwards, trying to process what I'm seeing. Thea sits upright, the movement swift, clean. My gears skip a frantic beat. This is not right. Then her pale eyes swivel. Her uncanny gaze locks onto mine. Her mouth opens as if to speak, but then she screams, the sound like that of gears shearing apart.

I watch as her metal skin begins to tarnish. Her silver and copper casings turn dull, the colours shifting to become ash-grey and brown. Green veins appear, etching themselves into her stained metal. She screams again, but this time it sounds almost human. Then her metal skin peels apart.

I watch in horror as the pistons and shock absorbers that constitute her skeleton are revealed. The exposure of her working parts is obscene. But worse still are the slowly growing sheets of flesh, seething and crawling to cover her.

Thea's body quivers, a response I recognise as pain, something no mechanical should feel. Then she falls still. The flesh stops growing. Her half-flesh, half-metal chest rises and falls as she gulps air into lungs she should not own.

Half metal, half flesh, her body is unfinished.

'Thea Unit?' My voice is rusty. I haven't used it in over a century.

The sound draws her gaze to mine.

I recoil from her human eyes; the watching of irises that contract and widen in the uncertain light of the cave. Slowly, gingerly, Thea swings her legs off the pallet. Real fingernails scrape against the timber as her fingers flex.

'Who are you?' she asks.

'Ena Unit,' I reply. 'Salvage, Search and Rescue.'

'Search and Rescue?' Thea laughs, a too-human sound.

My gears suddenly feel dry. I wish I could have another mouthful of oil.

Thea smiles, her once copper teeth are visible behind her flesh-pink lips. Her teeth look to be stained brown. 'So, did you search and rescue me? Salvage me?'

'Yes. Parts of you were salvaged from elsewhere in order to make you functional.'

Suddenly her voice is hard, unkind. 'You should have left me where I was.' She points at her chest. 'This body is an abomination.' Her face is set like stone; she looks as if she wants to attack me.

I take a step back. My heel catches the edge of an empty oilcan. It clatters away.

Thea pushes herself off the pallet. The skin-covered stumps of her wings hang uselessly by her side; two once-elegant sails now heavy with flesh.

I retreat further, watching as her metal parts—neck, patches of torso and one leg—catch and absorb the light. The rest of her body, the parts covered in flesh, is blushed pink.

'You idiot,' she says. 'You don't even know what you've done, do you?'

I feel the damp cave wall at my back. I can retreat no further. 'What I have done?'

Thea scoffs, her green eyes flare. 'I was a seeding drone,' she says, as if that admission explains everything.

'Yes. A DAx25 model,' I say. 'A cloud-seeding drone.'

'No.' The word hangs like acid in the air. 'I was modified. I was a human-seeding drone sent out by the Institute of Life for Humanity. The core-brain module you put in this body was full of human genomes.'

The green corrosion on the component suddenly makes sense. The module was leaking. That's why Thea's body remains incomplete: one hundred years of exposure had stolen part of the dose. There hadn't been enough left to effect a full change to the host body.

I try to explain, 'You—'

But she won't let me talk. 'No, it's you,' she says. 'You've wasted humanity's last shot at existence on this stupid metal body.'

I have no opportunity to explain. I watch Thea wheel away, her anger crackling like electricity. She stalks to the cave entrance, climbs out over the rocks and leaves. My programming screams at me to go after her, to save her, but there's another part of me that knows this world is no place for the living, and that it's already too late for Thea.

But I have to try.

I burst into action, my metal boots clanging and scraping against the rocks in my frantic effort to catch her. I clear the entrance to the cave, but misjudge my step. The rocks outside are slippery. My foot skids sideways and I tumble over a small ledge of ocean-battered rock. The sky and sea pinwheel in my field of view: blue, green, blue.

I'm lying wedged between two boulders with the sound of pounding surf roaring around me. Salt and sea foam sprays across my face. The buttery texture of oil coats my lips.

Diagnostics: I am damaged. Shattered leg. Crushed chest. Critical leak somewhere deep inside.

I need to get to the cave, to my surplus parts, but I can't get this body back alone.

I look around. And then I see her.

Thea is only metres away. She is sitting on a rock, her metal hand clutched to her chest. She is doubled over. I see her glance up. Her gaze catches mine. I see her cough. I can't hear the sound over the surf, but I see the sudden, bright spray of scarlet blood coat her lips and chin. Then, with herculean effort, she gets to her feet.

Her steps are unsteady as she navigates her way across to me. She says nothing as she grabs my wrist and begins to drag me out of the rocks. I try to help, using my good leg to kick myself free. Slowly she pulls me out, a sheen of oil slicking the water-wet rocks behind me in shades of blue, pink and green. My leg dangles, and sparks fly as she drags me further across the unforgiving terrain. The scrape of my metal skin over the stones is louder than the waves.

Thea gets me to the cave. Now inside, I can hear the heavy rasp of her breath as it struggles in and out of her half-formed lungs. I can feel her uneven pulse in the palm that grips my wrist so tightly. The human part of her is dying, but the mechanical in her is keeping her going, for the moment.

She drags me up onto the pallet. It's a struggle, but her android muscles have more strength than a human's. Once I'm laid out, she pauses for a moment, her head resting against my good leg. 'Damn it, but you're heavy.'

'I'm made of metal.'

She laughs, a tired sound. I watch as she reaches down. Her human hand closes over her own metal leg. A series of clicks and suddenly she pulls it free of her body. She braces herself against the pallet and places the leg on my chest.

'I can't,' she says.

So I sit upright, hold the spare leg and detach my damaged one. I click the new one into place just as Thea slides to the floor. While bad, the damage to my chest will have to wait. I recognise that Thea's need is now more urgent. I slip off the pallet and gently kneel by her side.

Her eyes flutter open. 'I'm sorry, Ena, I know this isn't your fault.' She coughs. More blood. 'These humans ... so many emotions ... so much pain.'

I want to understand, but my programming has limits. I have no reference for identifying how it feels to be human. So I do the only thing I can for her; the thing I once did for another. I sit next to her and hold her hand as she lies dying.

Long moments pass. The sound of waves swelling rumbles against the rocks outside, the wind whines.

Then Thea breathes a final, laboured breath. Her eyes close.

And just like that, I am alone again.

Omega.

The last.

And even with the noise of the sea around me, the silence of the world is suddenly deafening.

Tattoo

The tattoo burns every time I dream of him, that blue-eyed, blond-haired devil dressed in jeans and black leather jacket. It's his sharp blue eyes that frighten me the most. In the dream they glow, staring though me as if imploring me to remember something. But how can I? The Establishment wipes our memories to keep us focused.

But what if the phantom is right? What if I have indeed forgotten something important? All I know is that each time I see him, I wake, my chest tight with dread.

I'm awake now. I throw back the tangle of sweat-drenched sheets and turn on the bedside lamp. The glow illuminates the sparse room around me. Polished black walls and floor tiles, thin slab bed, matching side table and small alarm clock. Standard Establishment design. Even the lamp is minimalist, just a white stalk fitted to the table top with a curled half-leaf shade. Ugly.

The door to my ensuite is ajar. The thought of a shower is overwhelmingly tempting. I'm still dressed in last night's clothes and they smell of smoke and burnt metal. At least I kicked off my boots before falling into bed.

And the underside of my foot is still burning. I lift it and inspect the letters inked into the arch. They spell out four names.

David Bayer
Greer Bayer
Beau Bayer
Asher Bayer

The names mean nothing to me. My name is Nine, given because I am the ninth phantom hunter in the Establishment regiment. It's a name that's simple and easy to remember. Nothing fancy like the ones scribed beneath my foot.

I reach down and trace the lines of the tattoo with my fingertip. I wonder who they were, these four people. I wonder who, where, why and when their identities were inked into me. I don't know, but some deep-set part of me understands the tattoo should be kept hidden. The names are a secret. I've not even told the Establishment evaluator that they exist.

I ease my foot down onto the porcelain tiles. Their cool touch is pleasant and it eases the burning sensation.

Beside me the electric clock flicks from 5:59 am to 6:00 am. I push myself upright. I need to get ready. The evaluator will arrive soon with my new assignment, and experience has taught me never to make her wait.

* * *

The warm water from the shower runs through my hair and down over my breasts, easing the aches from the muscles I strained in last night's fight. The level-two phantom in the old building on Queen Street hadn't gone down easily. But then hardly any of them ever do.

Ghosts are even more desperate to cling to life than the living. Some of them fight. Hard. Some of them scream, and some of them just weep. We are trained by the Establishment to deal with these situations. Phantoms, they say, are just echoes: echoes that cannot speak, echoes of emotions no longer real. They are just memories refusing to fade.

Sometimes I'm not so sure, though. Sometimes killing them makes me feel like a murderer.

I close my eyes and rest my forehead against the fogged glass door. I feel as if I'm too old for my job, even though twenty-five isn't considered that old in most circles. I pick up the bar of soap and lather my body. The smell of sandalwood curls up around me as the streaks of ash and dirt are washed away. Scented soap is the one non-standard item I'm allowed to own. I'm not sure why, but I always choose sandalwood.

My fingers stumble over the raised ridges of flesh that scar my forearms, reminders of a lifetime of fighting phantoms. I have always found it interesting that an insubstantial-looking ghost can carve mortal flesh from bone with just a touch. And it hurts, too, the searing pain that's both hot and cold.

For my part, it takes more to kill a ghost than just a touch. It takes a gun modified to fire electricity and handfuls of powdered aluminium. The electricity binds them; the aluminium douses their spark. The thing is; it needs to be done before they get the chance to touch you.

I step free of the shower. The bathroom is filled with steam, the walls slick with droplets held suspended against gravity. I reach for the standard-issue grey towel hanging on the hook by the door. It's soft against my skin as I wipe away the water. I twist up my hair in the towel and secure the ends in a knot at the top.

I look into the mirror. Its silvered surface is ghosted over with a thin film of steam. I reach up. My fingers brush the surface, revealing my face …

And that of the blue-eyed devil standing behind me.

My heart lurches sideways as the room falls cold with his presence. The sheet of moisture on the mirror cracks as it is suddenly turned to ice. I pivot and fall into a crouch, reaching for the gun still tucked into my jacket lying on the floor. The grip is cold beneath my searching fingers. I latch onto it and pull it free. The bag of powered aluminium next to it falls open, spilling out like glitter across the floor.

The ghost takes a step back. I rise to my feet, the gun aimed and held firmly in my fist. But even armed, I'm aware that I'm facing this phantom naked, and it makes me feel exposed to him in more ways than one.

The blue-eyed phantom stands hesitant in the doorway, his hair glittering gold in the spilled light of the bathroom's heat lamp. He is wary, but his eyes are not on the gun. They are on me. The pale blue orbs stare through me into the secret place where my soul resides. They are as fierce in reality as they have ever been in my dreams. I see in them, as I have so many times before, the familiar plea.

Remember.

I remind myself that he's just an echo, an echo needing to be sent on his way.

I line him up in the gun's sight: a quick squeeze to bind him, aluminium dust to finish him off ... easy. I begin to squeeze the trigger—

'No. Wait!' says the phantom.

I halt.

Phantoms don't speak.

The tattoo beneath my foot begins to burn.

The ghost glances down at my foot and then back up to meet my eyes. 'It burns because it holds the memory for you. The memory that needs to be freed.'

Cold settles into the pit of my stomach. 'What memory?'

The ghost grows bolder. He takes a step toward me, crossing over the door threshold. My gun is the only barrier between us.

'Asher Bayer,' he says.

The world tips sideways. Somewhere in the distance, I feel my body slide to the floor. The gun falls from my lax grasp and skitters across the tiles. The ghost approaches, but I am helpless to retreat. He kneels over me and touches my forehead.

And suddenly I see.

His name is Beau Bayer.

'Asher.' His voice is a whisper in the maelstrom of memories that swirl around me.

* * *

I am five years old, holding my mother's hand as we pick purple flowers from the garden behind our house. She smells like sandalwood. Her name is Greer Bayer.

* * *

I am six and my father is bouncing me on his knee. I am laughing as he tickles me. David Bayer.

* * *

I am ten. The room is dark except for the light of a kerosene lamp. My father holds a tattoo needle dripping in black ink. *Red Fire Monkey* is printed on the side of the tool, the name of his tattoo parlour. My mother bids him to hurry. *Ink the names in quickly. It's the only way she'll remember us.* My father grasps my foot in his rough palm. There is a stinging pain as he presses the needle to my arch.

* * *

I am eleven and am being torn from my father's arms by men dressed in black. The evaluator stands by, watching, her smile an evil smudge on her red-painted lips. My mother is kneeling on the ground screaming. One hand reaches toward me, the other is held protectively around a young man who lies still on the footpath.

His blond hair glimmers gold in the evening light, his bright blue eyes stare sightlessly toward the sky. His jeans and black leather jacket are streaked with dirt and blood. He is dead. His name is Beau Bayer. He is my older brother.

I'm thrown back into my body with the force of a sledgehammer.

* * *

I gasp for air, feeling as if I've been starved of it for hours. My forehead stings where my brother has touched it. I feel the blood leaking down between my eyes. I'm slumped against the vanity unit, sprawled with all my nakedness clear to see.

Beau kneels next to me. I look into his eyes. They no longer seem fierce to me; instead they are filled with a sadness that transcends death.

A wry smile tugs at the corner of his lips. 'Welcome back, baby sister.' His face turns serious. 'You need to find the others.'

'What about you?'

'It's already too late for me.'

I hear a click, and I cry out as a lick of blue electricity coils around his shoulders. His eyes roll back into his head and his mouth opens in a silent scream. The air is suddenly filled with a glistening curtain of powdered aluminium. It touches him and turns to ash.

He becomes origami as, piece by piece, he is tucked closer into himself. In moments, he is reduced down to a single glowing star hovering above the tiles like a tiny sun. His spark. Then he winks out, and my brother is gone.

The figure of the evaluator replaces him. She is standing in the doorway, my own electric gun held in her right fist, a bag of powdered aluminium in the other. Her sharp red nails are curled around the weapon almost lovingly. Rumour has it that it's been some time since she hunted phantoms, but I see now in her face that the lust for it remains.

I lean forward and tuck my tattooed foot under my opposite knee. I now understand the danger in letting her see it. It wouldn't be just a memory wipe if she finds the tattoo, it would be brain alteration, just like she did to me when I was a child.

I remember the needles now, burrowing into my head, stealing away the faces of those I loved most in this world. The evaluator stole me from my family and turned me into her slave. A phantom hunter: a murderer who destroyed innocent spirits to protect Establishment secrets.

I'm sure the world would not look kindly upon their government condoning the killing and abduction of children. Maybe it's time the world was educated.

I keep my gaze locked onto the floor until I'm sure I can control the emotions that war within me. Then I look up at her. Her dark eyes glitter like two pieces of broken glass. I see the uncertainty in the lines of her face. She recognised Beau, I'm sure of it, and she's wondering if he spoke to me.

It's my turn to keep secrets now.

'Thank you, Evaluator,' I manage to say. 'The phantom caught me unawares.'

She glances down at my nakedness and then looks away. 'Did he speak to you, Nine?'

'Ma'am?' I try to look confused. 'Phantoms don't talk.'

Her face relaxes. 'Of course,' she says. 'Get up, I have a new assignment for you.' She flicks a piece of paper toward me. The sheet flutters down, a snow-white square on the ash-streaked ruin of my bathroom. I see two names penned on it. My heart stops mid-beat.

David Bayer
Greer Bayer

I look up at her.

She smiles. She looks like a shark. 'Rebel phantoms,' she says, 'haunting a building in the western suburbs. Particularly dangerous ones that I've been meaning for some time to put to rest.'

I can't help myself. 'Who were they?'

The evaluator tilts her head, evaluating me, no doubt. She, for some reason, decides to answer. 'Leaders of the Red Fire Monkey rebellion,' she says. 'Killed ten years ago for plotting to overthrow the Establishment. Their phantoms are stirring discord. Trying to reignite old fights. They need to be dealt with.'

I blink, wondering if she's testing me to see if I will react to the news of my parents' deaths. But it's not worth my life to let anything show. I swallow my anger. It takes everything I have to hold my expression impassive. I take my time, crumpling the piece of paper in my hand. I lift my chin.

'Of course, ma'am, I'll get dressed and head off right away.'

She scans my face a moment longer. I endure her stare, knowing she will find nothing. Finally, she nods and turns to leave.

As I watch her go, I think about the names inked into my foot. Beau's spirit is gone, sacrificed to deliver a message, but both Greer and David Bayer's remain. My mother. My father.

'I'm coming,' I whisper to them. 'I'll join the fight.'

The tattoo beneath my foot begins to burn.

The Memory Tree

Sixty years ago, I was born with a unique gift: the ability to take any memory and, for a short time, make it real. That's right, the literal recreation of memory into solid form. A true engagement of the senses: sight, taste, sound, smell and touch.

This supernatural skill is inherited from my mother's side of the family. Something to do with ancient gypsy bloodlines, I'm told. My mother, also born with the gift, has always held to the notion that it should be embraced, but I'm more cautious. To court the danger of never moving forward with life, always revisiting what has passed rather than focusing on what lies ahead …

I know from bitter experience where that can lead. But things have changed. Now, moving forward is not the concern; it's the past I'm interested in.

It's early morning, and the sun-tinted mist hovers low over the wide, coffee-brown stretch of river. I smile at the popping sound of fish lips breaking the surface as carp feed on their morning buffet of insects. The sound accompanies others; cricket chirrups and distant magpie carolling blend together to create a Murray River chorus.

I sit back against the lightning-scarred scribbly gum that clutches at the river's edge. Its exposed roots dangle over the eroded bank and dip gracefully into the calm water below. I take a breath, relishing the smells of rich earth, moist air and damp eucalyptus.

I close my eyes. I feel the strength of my gift hovering just beneath my skin. Engaging it is as easy as breathing. I let it sink in through the dark scribbly lines scrawled across the trunk of the tree at my back. Inside, among the ancient growth rings of timber, I find what I have come for: the scribbly gum's memory of the day the lightning struck.

I smile, triumphant. The tree not only remembers the strike, but it also remembers me standing beneath it at the time.

I let my muscles relax, easing myself into the meditative state that allows the memories to manifest. I feel my fingers begin to tingle ...

'Why such a serious face, sweetheart?'

I remember those words.

I open my eyes and there he is. Jacob. It's been forty years since I last saw his face.

Feelings I would rather not relive begin to crowd in upon me and I'm suddenly drowning in the emotional turmoil of my twenty-year-old self. But it's been a long time since I was that young. I steel my will and remind myself that what I'm feeling is only an echo of the past.

I steady my breath and force myself to look at Jacob. He is sitting beside me, his long lanky legs crossed in awkward disarray. He tilts his head and smiles. My heart skips a beat. His twenty-year-old face is the one I have seen in my dreams every night for as long as I can remember.

I take in the details of him with a hunger that surprises me: dark brown eyes, the mop of walnut-coloured hair, full lips and slightly pointed nose. My gift has rebuilt him to perfection. I resist the urge to reach out and touch him. I'm not ready yet.

His smile turns down slightly on one side, creasing his cheek into a dimple. 'What's wrong?' he asks.

I'm surprised that he doesn't seem to notice how old I am. But then again, I've never explored the full potential of my gift and don't understand its parameters exactly. Perhaps when refabricating memories, the people in them see you as you were then, too.

'I just wanted to speak to you,' I reply.

'About what?'

I hesitate. I know there's no harm in changing the memory, but I always feel disappointed knowing that the reality outside of it remains constant. I know that whatever is said here today, outside of this construct I will still be slowly dying.

'I want to talk about death.'

Jacob's brow furrows. 'Death?' he says. 'Why discuss that on such a beautiful day?'

I force myself to speak again, worried that I will lose the courage to do so if I hesitate any longer. 'I'm dying.' It's the first time that I've said the words out loud. I've been hoping that by avoidance I could somehow outrun fate.

His face creases with worry. Any semblance to my original memory of this day is gone. 'What are you talking about?'

'Cancer,' I say. 'I don't have long now.'

'What? When?' I hear the sudden, urgent desperation in his voice; he doesn't want to lose me.

I fill my smile with my sadness. 'They've done all they can.'

'What about—'

'No.'

'Is there—'

'No.'

His objections falter. 'What can I do?'

'Only one thing.'

'Name it,' he says.

'Tell me if you would keep the promise.'

He pauses before answering, teasing at his bottom lip with his teeth. He knows the promise I mean. 'You want to know whether, if I were to die first, I would wait for you at the gates of heaven. That promise?'

'Yes.'

'You already know the answer to that.'

'Humour me.'

His eyes soften. He lifts his hand and brushes his fingers down the side of my face. The touch is like ice against my skin, my gift unable to simulate the true warmth of human touch. I shudder, but do not pull away. I'm happy to endure the discomfort.

'I would wait a million years for you if I had to,' he says.

Tears, hot and salty, spill from my eyes and track their way down my wrinkled cheeks. I reach out and touch his cold face in return. I've heard what I came to hear. I release my focus. His form fractures and blows away like tattered threads of fabric.

With him gone, old grief reawakens. My heart feels as if it has stopped beating. I sit for a moment, wiping at tears that refuse to stop falling, all for a memory now four decades old.

We had been here alone that day, Jacob and I. Young and in love, with the thought of ever being apart a terrible torment. Our promise had been made by the edge of the river, the words sealed with a kiss beneath the old scribbly gum. I remember feeling like we were living a lifetime in that moment.

Then a brilliant flash of light and I woke up in hospital a week later. The lightning had struck us from a clear blue sky. I survived, but Jacob did not.

At first I used my gift to hide among my memories of him. A million times over, I relived that day, changing the memory so that Jacob survived. But at night my dreams betrayed me, always reminding me of the truth. I became a hermit living in the darkness of my room, haunted by whispers I wasn't sure were entirely real. Family and friends all thought me mad, and perhaps for a short while I was.

Clarity finally came in the form of my mother, who, having grown concerned at my abuse of the gift, intervened. She pointed out that Jacob had saved my life that day by taking the full force of the lightning strike instead of me. She said that I was selfish to waste his sacrifice. Her words had angered me initially, but eventually I saw the wisdom in them. Jacob would have wanted me to live.

And so I gave up using the gift, focusing instead on living the life he had saved for me. But a career, a husband and three children later, I still find myself asking: *Why did he have to die?*

I get to my feet, steadying myself against the tree. Oddly, my legs feel more stable than they have in a long time. I don't feel so sick, either, or even so old. I brush loose grass from my pants. I glance up one last time at the scribbly gum, taking in the ragged lines of its shattered crown against the early-morning sky. I commit its earthy beauty to memory, for I don't expect to ever pass this way again.

I feel a warm hand gently touch my shoulder.

'Where are you going, sweetheart?'

I gasp. I turn around. It's Jacob, but he is no fabrication. The warmth of his hand tells me so.

'What are you doing here?' I ask, shocked.

'I've been here for some time,' he says. 'Waiting.'

I glance down at my hands; my skin is no longer aged, my fingers are finely tapered. I look up at him. We relive a lifetime in a moment.

Metamorphosis

The hems of my trousers mire in the soft sand as I run barefoot over this wild beach; this graveyard for whales. It makes my passage slow, and being slow will mean my death. My sweat smells like fear and my lungs burn with my frantic intake of salt-tinged air. My pursuers are close behind, but they are yet concealed behind the dunes. I hear their footsteps. They are hushed whispers through the seagrass.

It was a legend, told in the orphanage of my youth that brought me, a poor whaling captain, to this forsaken place. A promise of seas teeming with whales. Twelve months ago I left England aboard my *Agatha* with thirty crewmen. Two days ago, five of us landed on this beach in search of food and water. Now I wish we had never left England.

White sand, whalebone, and buttresses of tumbled stone stretch for miles ahead of me. Out against the horizon, *Agatha* rests quietly at anchor just outside the break in the reef. I see small figures, the remainder of my crew, scuttling about her rigging. My safety lies with the ship, if only I can reach her. I am so close.

The small whaleboat that brought me to land lies just ahead. It lies tilted on the sand, the idle repose of a vessel patiently awaiting the return of her captain. But I also see the rippled sand around her hull. Dark patches stain the pristine canvas. Old blood. That of the crew who landed with me and fell in those first few violent minutes that followed.

I try not to remember how the lizard people cut apart the bodies of my men before hauling them up into the village behind the dunes, or how I was made to watch as they feasted upon them with shark-like teeth. Why they kept me alive I'll never know, but one thing is certain: the sound of human bone cracking between their jaws will haunt me forever.

But if it hadn't been for their gorging, they wouldn't have fallen asleep and I might not have slipped my bonds and escaped.

I grasp the anchor rope and pull it free of the sand. I lean into the bow of the whaleboat and try to push. My feet skid and slide on the slick sand, but the hull remains stubbornly lodged.

A now familiar keening draws my attention: the sound of my captors. I look over my shoulder. A wave of them crest the top of the closest dune, spears brandished like a thicket of thorns. Their hairless, scaled skin glitters green in the sunlight, and even from this distance I see their shark teeth glittering white behind black lips peeled back to thin lines.

I turn. I run.

The sand is firmer closer to the water. It's easier going. But the creatures are not far behind. I choke on a sob. I don't want to die like this.

I round an outcrop of rock. Ahead, sprawled at the waterline, is the cottage-sized carcass of a whale calf. Sperm whale. The body lays two-thirds in the water, as if the tide beached it only moments ago. I capture the details of it in a moment: the skin mottled white and grey, the hole torn in the animal's side.

The opening is large and fringed with flaps of tattered flesh. Blue-grey guts spill from it, the roped coils of intestine slithering and sliding across the sand, in cadence to the motion of the waves. Out beyond, in the deeper water between the beach and *Agatha*, I see whale spume gust into clear sky. The mother whale lingering for her lost calf? I feel a moment of jealousy. If only my mother hadn't died before she had the chance to show such devotion to me.

The thought is torn away by a spear piercing my leg. I cry out and stumble. I fall only metres from the carcass. Reaching back, I fear I will faint as I tear the spear free, but I don't. My blood is bright against the sand. I try to stem the flow. I hear the lizard people cheer. Their cry chills me to the core. I begin to crawl toward the whale carcass.

Up close, the smell of dead whale is overpowering. I gag as I enter the water, ignoring the feel of loose innards coiling around my wrists. The waves are freezing. The hide of the whale is slimy. It pulls away as I grasp the side of the wound in the stomach. I slip the first time.

Waves buffeting me, I reach up again. This time I find the solid edge of an exposed rib. I drag myself up and in. My chest slithers over the edge of the hole and finally I'm within the whale. I look down. My blood is mixing with the seawater lying in the bottom of the whale's body cavity.

Outside, I hear the lizard people's jubilant cheers change to frantic screeching. I hear the slap of their feet against the wet sand.

Desperate, I crawl upwards, closer to the head of the animal. The light is weaker up here and I must lie flat on my stomach to fit, but somehow I feel safer. I try to tuck my legs up closer to my chest, but I can't. They suddenly seem wedged in tight against the spine of the whale. I arch my back, but it feels stiff, as if it's fused to the whale.

The grey light filtering in behind me disappears. I'm enveloped in darkness, total and complete. Nausea rises in my gut. I squeeze my eyes shut and then open them again.

There is light. I realise I am seeing out of the whale's eyes.

No, I think.

I *am* the whale.

The lizard people surround me. Their spears, tipped with wicked barbs, are poised to plunge into the new flesh grown over the ragged hole in my side. I arch my back. My tail thrashes. Seawater churns to foam.

The creatures hedge around me, wary. Instinctively I know they fear me. I lash my tail again and the resulting wave sends several of the creatures flying. Their elongated limbs look like flotsam as they crumple, dashed against the beach.

Pain blooms on my right side. I scream. The sound comes out strangely, like a long drawn-out note of music. I swivel my whale eye to look back; it's difficult because my head does not move as it once did. I catch a glimpse of the end of the spear that has pierced my side.

I thrash my tail again. I slide deeper into the water. The saltwater stings as it seeps in around the wound. I wriggle again and the spear falls free of my flesh. The pain eases.

I thrash again and the lizard people retreat up the beach. I feel cool water flow over my head. Free of the sand, I am suddenly weightless. I ease away from the beach and head for deeper water, for *Agatha*. She floats at anchor, a lazy list tilting her timbered sides.

I surface next to her, calling out for my remaining crew. 'Drop the ladder. Haul me aboard.'

But I have forgotten I'm a whale, and it is only with the whale's voice that I speak. Still, my whale song draws attention.

I look up. The sides of my ship are lined with green-scaled creatures.

My heart drops. My remaining crew is dead, no doubt.

The ship's whaleboats are lowered over the side. They bristle with creatures holding spears at the ready. I know they intend to hunt me down.

A shadow emerges from the depths below me. A monstrous wedge-shaped head, dappled with quivering rays of filtered sunlight rises, faster and faster. Her skin is marked with scars and crusted over with barnacles.

It is the mother whale, and with her comes the weight of her ire. She swims past me and I'm buffeted aside by the force of her passage. Her broad head slams into the underside of the first boat and the creatures within are flung skyward. They fall, slamming into the ocean amidst a cauldron of bubbles. They try to swim, but their reptilian hands are not made for the job.

I'm not sure what compels me to approach them, but I do. Perhaps it is a remnant of my humanity that calls for revenge. I gather the lizard people into my mouth one by one. I bite down, relishing the feel of their bones cracking between my jaws.

The mother whale is done with the whaleboats. Her attention has turned to the ship. She approaches it, gaining speed before

63

ramming it broadside. The squeal of broken timbers carries through the current to where I wait. The sailor in me laments the loss of my ship, but the whale in me knows it must be done.

The mother whale floats, stunned for a moment, then turns and rams *Agatha* again. This time her timbers break and seawater pours in through the breach. Barrels, harpoons and lengths of uncoiled ropes topple into the water. They float a moment before the currents catch them and bear them away. The ship settles deeper into the water. She seems to pause for a moment, and then slides bow first beneath the waves. Her masts resemble the crosses that humans place over their graves.

I feel a nudge against my side and find the mother whale floating next to me. Her eye fixes onto mine.

Thank you for your sacrifice, she communicates to me, her song an ancient melody carried on the salty current.

Sacrifice?

Yes. The life force you sacrificed for my son to swim again.

I look into the deep blue distance and watch the underside of the waves that ripple in the world overhead. For a moment I am both whale and man, and understand the ultimate irony of my fate: a lifetime spent hunting whale, only to become one.

I look around. There is beauty in this world beneath the waves. And in the mother by my side, I have found the family I never had.

I feel no regret as I let the human part of me slide away. I turn, happy to cling close to my mother's side as she leads us toward deeper water. I know it to be a wild ocean we head for. An ocean that shifts ceaselessly over white sand that stretches for miles into the distance.

The Darkness Has Teeth

It's 11:30 pm, if the watch on my wrist is working correctly. A full moon, burning orange, hangs low on the distant horizon. A ruined highway stretches out before me. As I walk, my boots catch the edges of broken bitumen, but I ignore the distraction. My mind is elsewhere. At midnight, I will have another chance to travel back through time, another chance to put things right.

My fingers toy with the weapon concealed inside my pocket. The knot of tension in my chest is the size of a fist. I've failed so many times.

A derelict house emerges out of the night, two storeys high. It clings to the side of the highway like a pale ghost. The roof is shattered, tiles fallen away to reveal broken trusses. Twin verandas smile at me crookedly with their gap-toothed balustrades; the once ornate windows behind them are shadowed.

I pause at the bottom of the splintered staircase leading up to the first-storey veranda. I scratch at my beard, looking up at the old wicker chairs lying tumbled about, broken and crumbling.

Dust covers everything. No footprints mar the even surface, but that means nothing. The things I fear don't always leave footprints.

Dust billows around my ankles as I take the four steps. Everything is quiet. I make my way to the door, which, like the roof, is shattered. But this time, it's the embedded shotgun pellets in the doorframe that tell the story. Someone once made a final stand here.

I brush past the door and splinters catch in the cuff of my jacket. I flick them away. I take a breath. I cross the threshold.

Inside, the foyer is dim. A fallen barricade of furniture spills out across the floor. My gaze sweeps the room.

More furniture. A ragged old rug.

A male corpse, shotgun held in lax fingers.

The perfectly intact body lies fallen like a broken doll against a sofa. I shudder. I hate how bodies don't decompose anymore. Demon toxins. The poison preserves the flesh. And the affected lie where they fall, that is, until their bodies are needed again.

I step closer. Thin moonlight streaming in through a window reveals his features to me: white hair, wrinkled skin, and blue eyes staring sightlessly into the distance. He has the look of an old-timer, possibly one of the original sugarcane farmers who dwelt in these parts.

I take another step. The corpse doesn't move: a good sign. I see an old leather wallet sprawled open on the floor. The licence reads *John Everton*. I wish I hadn't seen it. Knowing the man's name only adds to my burden of guilt. My mistakes are why old John is lying here dead.

I turn my attention back to the fallen barricade. The haphazard array of furniture lies across an open doorway that leads further back into the house. The rooms beyond it stand dark. I reach into my pack, pull out my torch and turn it on. Climbing over more wicker furniture, I push a small desk to one side and step through the doorway.

Beyond the opening is a hall. The floor, walls and chandeliers are layered thick with dust. I flick my torch over each surface, looking for the cracks I hope aren't there. My initial sweep reveals nothing, but any fissures could still be hidden.

I lift my boot and thud it hard against the floor. The old timbers groan in protest. Then slowly the dust covering the gaps between the boards begins to filter away. There are cracks, all right. Many.

I back slowly out of the doorway, past the desk and back over the wicker furniture. I try to do so quietly, but the hard rubber soles of my boots scuff, and each scrape sets my teeth on edge.

Then I hear it.

The sound of the demons; the sound of their black tar bodies slithering out of the cracks and crawling over the floor.

I move fast. I'm back in the foyer. My breathing is shallow. I swing the light of my torch in a blue-white arc around the room. It passes over the couch, flicks past the window, washing out the spill of moonlight. It falls on the doorway leading outside to fresh air and freedom … and there in the opening stands John Everton's corpse, now animated, shotgun loaded and ready.

I should never have come in here.

The corpse snarls at me. His teeth glitter yellow in the beam of my torch. His silver hair shines white and his eyes are now two orbs of darkness. I can see the demon behind them, the one that's taken up residence in his empty head.

It's smiling.

It's anticipating dinner.

Me.

The cracked glass in the window shatters as I plough my shoulder into it. I slither out over the sill and land hard on the gravel below. I struggle to my feet and turn to run.

I pull up short, halted by the business end of a double-barrelled shotgun aimed at my head.

John Everton's now black eye has me lined up in the gun's sight. I stare straight back into it—that pool of midnight ink. From the corner of my own eye, I see his trigger finger twitch, but before he can pull it a shrill electronic beeping sounds out. I glance down.

My watch.

It's midnight. And with midnight comes the magic.

The electric crackle of the time portal forming makes my hair stand on end. A torrent of wind kicks up, blasting static dust into clouds. John Everton staggers backwards. His gun shifts to aim uselessly at the sky. Then the portal burgeons into life, a ring of blue fire engulfing me, drawing me down and drowning me in light.

* * *

I open my eyes and instinctively know I am fifteen years old. I am lying flat on a perfect green lawn, the sun shining down on me from above. Behind me is the house I just escaped from, but it now appears well maintained. In the distance, fields full of gently waving sugarcane ripple in a soft, warm breeze.

I reel. I forget how striking the world was before I ruined it.

I sit up and look down at my watch. I press the button on the side, setting the alarm. Fifteen minutes before the portal resets and I'm sent back. Not long, but hopefully it's enough time.

I get to my feet and reach into my pocket. The weapon is not much to look at. It's a slender metal cylinder I made to be as thin and long as a pencil. Inside it, I have harnessed a spark of time taken from within the portal. The cylinder burns cold in my hand, the ember within heavy with the weight of history.

This all began with a small fissure in a rock, a crack that I used time to force wider. A terrible mistake made almost thirty years ago.

I walk around the side of the house and follow the gravel path leading to the back. My thoughts hover, insistent, at the forefront of my mind. The mistake.

I remember being twelve when it happened, too young to understand what using my mind to manipulate the flow of time would do. I didn't mean to widen the cracks of the world, didn't mean to stretch their fabric so thin as to create infinite doorways to a dimension of darkness. But the fact remains: I flooded the world with demons. Now all I want is to send the bastards back.

The gravel gives way to lush garden. The quiet trickling of water over rocks draws my attention. I dig through a hedge of gardenia bushes and find the small fountain and pond nestled at their centre. Goldfish hang lazy in the water, long tails brushing at the waterlily stems.

To one side of the pond, I see what I'm looking for: a large granite boulder. Its mossy green surface is dappled with sunlight;

a small swallow sits on top of it flicking its head from side to side as it searches for insects. Most importantly, the rock's rugged bulk is split nearly in two.

It's perfect.

I'm aware that time is ticking by. I run to the boulder and peer into the crack. Within it, I see the darkness I awoke all those years ago. It struggles within the fissure, trying to climb out, but in this window of time it still hasn't found the strength to break free.

I jam the pencil-thin cylinder into the crack. I press the release button on the end. The clawed end opens and the spark of time harnessed within descends into the crevice. I see the darkness recoil from the blue light, curling and seething like boiling tar. It looks just like it did on that day so long ago when it broke free of the cracks.

I remember it flooding out, hungry, searching for any sentient consciousness it could claim, and how its evil spread, rising to infect the sky, hiding the sun from us. Across continents, millions died. Their bodies still litter the streets of cities and towns alike. All empty vessels, a macabre sort of discarded clothing, non-decaying bodies awaiting a dark demon's consciousness to claim them for reanimation.

The blue spark floats deeper into the rock, the thin crevice lit by its brilliance. I see the darkness pull back further, but there's nowhere left for it to go. I step back. The crack glows bright blue for an instant and then the spark is quenched.

I hear crickets in the garden. I hear the trickle of water over worn rock.

Then the granite boulder explodes.

70

Splinters of rock shower down around me, along with puddles of black goop that writhe and seethe as they hit the grass. The puddles meld together, moving unnaturally fast to coalesce.

Failure.

Again.

And worse, the darkness is now free to hunt me.

'Shit!'

I turn and run. My feet fly over the shrubs and onto the gravel path. I hear sloshing behind me.

The demons.

They are hungry.

I skid around the front of the house. I see an old man working in the garden. I almost stop in my tracks. White hair, wrinkled skin and blue eyes: it's John Everton, the real John as he was in the days before he was killed.

'Whoa there, son, go easy,' he says as he notices me rounding the corner of the house. 'What's the rush?'

'Run!' I manage to gasp, but he doesn't.

His brow wrinkles in confusion. 'It's all right, Gwenda here will fix whatever's ailing ya.' He reaches down and picks up an old shotgun. I recognise the weapon. It's the one his corpse was holding back in my future. And while his bravery is admirable, the weapon will never hold back the demons.

'Get inside!' I scream as I veer past him, heading for the house.

My tone moves him to action. Still holding the gun, he turns and sprints, easily catching up to me. He's spry for an old man. We take the veranda steps together, two at a time. The front door is open, the foyer beyond welcoming. In moments, we are inside. I slam the door shut.

'What is it?' John's voice is a whisper.

But I have no chance to answer. The foyer turns dark as the black tar crawls over the glass windowpanes.

'Dear God.' John stares at the white, razor-edged teeth within the darkness pressed against the glass.

The glass cracks—a short, sharp sound—but the pieces hold in the frame, at least for the moment. There is scratching at the door, serrated claws and teeth hidden in the tar gouge at the timber. Soon the dark demons find their way in.

Their tar spreads like ink across the polished timber floor. The stain grows quickly, pulsing its way toward us. John, still holding the gun, starts to pull wicker furniture forward to barricade the doorway leading to the corridor. I grab a polished timber desk and drag it to the pile. The tar has almost reached us. I jump up onto the desk. I grip John's wrist and try to help him up, but a lick of tar grabs him by the ankle. I pull harder, but my grip slips. He falls backwards, landing heavily against a couch. The gun discharges accidentally, the spray of hot lead catching the entry door and frame, blasting pieces of wood outwards.

'Help!' John's face contorts with pain. 'They're eating me!'

They're not eating him, but I know what he means. Savage white teeth are piercing his skin, injecting toxins and drawing out his human consciousness.

I leap off the desk and onto the clear patch of floor by his side. I grasp his hand, trying to pull him away, but as I do a curl of tar takes firm grip upon my arm.

My watch alarm sounds.

Time is up.

'No!'

The time portal forms around me; the demons are too close.

I feel myself being sucked in. Then the ring of blue fire tears me from this sunlit world and transports me back to my own.

But in transit something feels different.

I open my eyes. To my horror, I see licks of darkness threaded through the blue fire of the portal corridor. The demons are in the portal. My panic inspires action. I spread out my fingers and let the threads catch on my fingertips. A trailing mess of darkness tangles around my hand. I ball it up, ignoring the sharp sting of serrated claws.

I am dropped out onto gravel. I turn, shielding my eyes against the portal's brightness with one hand and holding the dark demons in the other. As it begins to fade, I focus my mind and with it twist the axis of the portal. The time loop shifts and a new doorway is torn through reality and into limbo.

With all my strength, I hurl the ball of demons into the portal. A shriek echoes as I fall backwards.

Darkness.

* * *

I am back in my own time. Patterns of light are playing across my closed eyelids. A fresh breeze pulls at my fringe. I don't remember ever feeling so safe. I don't want to open my eyes. I am tired of the running, the hiding, the fighting. If I must die, let it be like here, like this.

I hear footsteps crunching over gravel.

'Can I help you there, son?' asks a familiar voice. 'You're squashing my pansies, lying there like that.'

I open my eyes. To my surprise, I find myself lying in a flowerbed, looking up through the gently swaying branches of a weeping willow. I turn my head. My gaze meets twinkling blue eyes.

John Everton.

'You all right?' His kind face is filled with sympathy.

I struggle upright. 'Sorry,' I manage to say, 'I, ah ...'

The old man smiles. 'It's all right. I've had a few benders in my time, too. Sometimes you just gotta sleep it off where you fall.'

John helps me to my feet. I am still in shock. I don't know whether to laugh or cry. Did I really succeed this time? Have the demons really gone? I look around at the impossibly beautiful day. Yes. I think so.

I let John lead me inside, his offer of bacon and eggs for breakfast too tempting to refuse. The foyer of the house is bright and warm when we enter. John directs me to a bathroom just off the corridor.

I realise it's been a long time since I saw my own face. When I look in the mirror I barely recognise the middle-aged man with brown eyes that have seen too much of life. Grey hair falls across my forehead and my beard is long. I look like the homeless man I am.

I reach over and turn on the basin tap. Clean, fresh water gurgles from the chrome spout, over the cracked porcelain and into the drain.

Cracked porcelain.

I freeze.

I lean down and peer into the crack.

Something black is struggling to get out.

The River Deep

The river is deep here, the water cold. But the rain is much colder. It beats against my forehead as I struggle to keep my nose above the waterline. Over me, the midnight storm rages on, the charcoal sky a stretch of undulating cloud flecked through with lightning.

My eyes hurt. I can taste motor oil. The houseboat that was my prison is gone, and so are the criminals on board. I wish I could see something. Anything. But there is only water and darkness. My nightie drags at me, my arms burn. Gravity finally prevails and the dark river water closes over my head.

My lungs are flooding. I panic, kick out and claw at nothing. But my sense of direction is gone.

One final kick and I know I'm done for. At least it's a far better fate than the one my kidnappers had planned for me.

The river is deep here, but I no longer feel cold. I'm drifting beneath the turmoil that rides above. Darkness crawls at the edge of my vision. I see refracted lightning rimed against the underside of the waves. I close my eyes and let go.

Thoughts of my family slide by: my father, the corrupt senator, and my mother, who supports his sociopathic drive for power. And what a drive for power it is; a drive that often upsets the wrong kind of people, the kind of people who would kidnap a man's daughter.

But even so, until recently I had thought my parents loved me. I'd heard the kidnappers talk about how he refused to pay the ransom for me. 'She'll die for his stubbornness,' one had said, 'and they'll never find her body.'

The current pulls me along. Winding tendrils of reeds curl around my ankles, submerged roots brush at my fingertips. I wonder for a moment where my kidnappers are and then the thought passes. Their fate is their own. As is mine.

I feel something sharp scrape down my arm and suddenly there is hope. My fingers grasp and meet the rugged end of a thick branch. Desperately, I clutch at it, clinging on for dear life. Then I'm being pulled through the water with it. I kick towards the bank. I feel mud and grass slither against my chest, and suddenly I am free of the river.

I'm lying on the rain-drenched riverbank. I feel the lash of raindrops. Then my lungs rebel and I vomit water. Air never tasted so good. Gradually my breaths come easier, but they still hurt. I can't believe I'm alive.

I turn to look for my rescuer. Standing over me, outlined in silver by the storm, is a bear-like creature standing upright on two legs. I recoil. My fingernails dig into the soft mud-lined bank. I scramble backwards. My cotton nightie tears against an exposed tree root.

The uncertain darkness reveals small details of the creature's face: a momentary glint of green eyes, a curtain of dark, wet hair. The creature lifts its hand; the long fingers are tipped with black claws.

The savage hands reach for me. I squeal and struggle, the hands retreat.

Then the creature's shadowed face leans into mine. Guttural words, spoken low, reach my ear. 'I'm a friend.' The voice is undeniably male.

As the man steps back, I see that his hands are not clawed at all, but are holding a forked tree branch—the branch helped pull me from the water. Suddenly I'm uncertain. Does he truly mean me no harm?

It makes no difference, I decide. I'm alone on an unknown stretch of river. What choice do I have? The man must sense my resignation for he reaches out for me again. This time I let him gather me into his arms. He lifts me clear of the mud and carries me away. I am lulled as the sound of the storm subdues, prevailed over by the dense Australian bush. I suddenly feel worn beyond endurance. I close my eyes and lean my forehead against my saviour's sodden chest. He smells like wet eucalyptus and teatree.

* * *

I am woken by sunlight on my eyelids. I open my eyes and find myself lying beneath a tree, cocooned in a bed of green leaves. I smell woodsmoke and roasting meat.

I push myself upright. There's a sharp pain in my forearm, and my throat and lungs feel raw. I glance down. Two long, bloodied scratches mark my skin. Scratches from the tree branch used to pull me to shore. They are not deep.

I am suddenly reminded. Where is the man?

I look around, but I'm alone. Nearby, a smokeless fire crackles merrily. Next to it, impaled on a smouldering tree branch, is a roasting rabbit carcass. My stomach gurgles. The meat smells good. And I bet it will taste even better.

I'm at the fireside in moments, my fingers pulling at the succulent meat. I tear free a leg. The flesh is savoury, the rich taste filling both my mouth and nostrils. I close my eyes and sigh with relish.

I hear the creak of a tree branch bending. I turn, eyes wide.

He strides confidently from beneath a heavy fall of she-oak branches. He is dressed in threadbare cotton pants and a faded blue shirt. A small insignia with the letters *GM* is embroidered in yellow cotton on the top left pocket.

The previous week in the company of evil men has taken its toll on me. I feel my muscles tense. I'm afraid, but I sense that running would be a mistake. Instead, I take a breath and hold out the rabbit leg. 'Thank you for breakfast.'

The man slows. He looks surprised, as if he hadn't expected me to be awake yet. In the morning light, I see that he's well built, muscled. And he's young, perhaps in his early thirties. Close to my age.

'Your name?' he asks.

'Maia Thorne.'

The man nods and moves a few steps closer. 'Tom.' His long hair hangs like limp rope down each side of his bearded face.

His green eyes are like chipped emerald. Those eyes. They carry fierceness in them. 'Where are you from, Maia?' His voice, while guttural, is cultured.

'I was being held prisoner on a houseboat that sank in the storm. You saved me. Thank you for that.'

Tom's features turn grim. 'No thanks needed,' he says. 'They were bad men, those that held you. But they can't hurt you anymore.'

I suddenly feel cold. 'What do you mean?'

'Come with me.'

Tom leads me away from camp and into the bush. He seems part of the landscape as he moves, his footsteps silent. He navigates with ease around trees and over logs. He goes fast and it takes all my effort to keep up with him. My focus is such that I almost jump out of my skin when a kookaburra starts laughing from a nearby tree.

Tom half turns at the sound, and I see the shadow of a smile on his sharp-edged profile. 'Just a kookaburra,' he assures me. 'She won't hurt you.'

I wish I could be sure. I'm a city girl born and bred. I don't know much about wildlife.

Soon, I hear the sound of wind over water. The ground becomes boggier, dry grass giving way to a damper sort of vegetation. Then the bush recedes and we're standing on the banks of the river.

And it is beautiful. I had seen nothing of it from my windowless cabin on the houseboat. The water ripples gently in the morning sun. Trees—gumtrees, teatree and an assortment of others—huddle at the water's edge. Their motley grey, white and orange trunks are a riot of texture backed by a canvas of dusky green leaves.

But the beauty is marred. Just ahead, cradled by the water at the river's edge, is the rotted wreck of an old, wooden-hulled paddle steamer. She lays on the bank, half in the water and half out. Vegetation drapes her sides like sodden paper. Her deck lines are blurred by time, weather and mud. The paddle boxes that once drove her sit just clear of the water. The mouldering timbers are a reminder of a river industry long faded into the past.

'What's that?' I ask Tom.

He shrugs. 'The *Gloria May*, once the finest paddle steamer on the Murray River. She sank in a storm, much like your houseboat.' Then he points across the river. 'Look.'

I follow the line of his finger. Nestled in the greenery on the opposite bank is the white outline of a shattered fibreglass boat. The torn lines of its hull sit nestled against the muddy bank. The name *Roaring Laines* is painted in strong black letters on the side. I recognise the houseboat.

I look at Tom.

'And there,' he says.

Again I follow the line of his finger. This time it's pointed down our side of the river. Three more shapes lie in the water, smaller than the broken carcass of the houseboat.

Bodies. Three pale, bloated corpses float among the tree roots that hang exposed over the bank. I recognise one by his dark beard: my kidnappers. All of them. Dead.

The sight of them turns my stomach and I twist away. But even without looking, the image of them remains: the exact hue of their blue lips, eyes eaten out by fish. I clutch at my stomach, dry retching.

But Tom lacks any sign of compassion. His voice is hard. 'They were bad people,' he repeats. 'They deserve to be gone.'

'No one deserves to die.'

'And yet dying is inevitable. It's who we are when we go that matters.'

'What would you know about it?'

Tom's gaze locks onto mine. 'The innocent remain. The corrupt disappear. These men?' Tom points at the bodies. My gaze involuntarily moves back to them. 'Their souls were not worth saving.'

'But—'

Tom's voice softens. 'Maia. They were corrupt and you are not. And so they are gone and you remain.'

Then Tom takes me by the hand. He leads me away from the bodies, following the line of the river. We pass the *Gloria May* again and head around a slight bend in the bank. An old, scarred gumtree comes into view, its dead trunk shining silver-grey in the sunlight. From one of the lower branches hangs the tattered remnant of a chain, a broken hangman's noose marring the end. And beneath it lies scattered bones, a skull grinning.

'Who is that?'

Tom looks solemn. 'There lies Captain Thomas Angus Burne,' he says. 'The *Gloria May* was his paddle steamer. It sank during a storm in July 1865. He survived on the banks of this river until he happened across a gang of bushrangers who hung him from that tree with a mooring chain.' Tom points to the bones beneath the noose. 'Then left his body there to rot.'

My story makes me feel sick, but it's the date the catches my attention. '1865?'

'Yes.'

'That was over a hundred and forty years ago.'

'Yes.'

'And how do you know the captain's story if he was never found?'

'I know because I was there.'

The taste of roast rabbit rises in the back of my throat. 'Tom?'

'Yes?'

'Is your last name Burne?'

Tom smiles a sad smile. 'It is,' he says.

A ridiculous thought crosses my mind. I feel stupid saying it out loud. 'Are you … a ghost?'

Tom's smile fades. 'Perhaps. Or maybe I'm just an innocent man who remains.'

Then he points at something caught in the roots of the hanging tree. It's another body, that of a slim-brown-haired woman. 'Just like she was once innocent and now remains.'

I dread the answer to my next question. 'Who was she?'

'You don't recognise her?'

I'm desperately trying to ignore the fact that she looks like me. 'Maia?'

I feel sick. My stomach has dropped to my feet. The truth is clear.

In the distance, I hear the kookaburra laugh again. I'm sure it's laughing at me.

Blue Moon

Ragged shadows stretch down from the small opening overhead. The shadows on the wall above me, and the thin slit of light from beneath the door are all I can see. I can hear strains of music outside. They are sharp, beautiful and deadly, just like the angelic faces of the creatures that hold me prisoner here. Or perhaps the creatures are devilish. I have been here so long, I can't remember anymore.

I sit as I always sit in my prison, cross-legged on the floor in front of the door, shoulders brushing the walls on each side. The door is the only way out, but it is sealed.

I try to remember the feel of the moonlight on my skin, the wind at my back, and something else: the face of a woman whose name I cannot recall, and something about a witch. But lately recollections have started to slip. I despair at the loss, but what can I do? Time and this endless incarceration are stealing even the memory of my memories from me.

I let my finger trace the slit of moonlight that seeps in along the bottom edge of the door. It is my nightly ritual, to sit and follow the line of light that joins the manmade cement floor to the pixie-wrought metal door. The silver alloyed into the metal burns my fingers, but the pain is a good pain. The pain reminds me that I am alive. It gives me hope.

But while the door burns me, the concrete is always ice cold. The touch of it is soothing against my scalded fingertips, the random pattern of its surface comfortingly familiar. Bump, dip, crack, rock …

The rock moves beneath my fingers. The rock being loose is new.

I shift closer. It's wedged against the bottom corner of the door. I wriggle it, wincing as my knuckles graze the metal. The stone gives way and with it comes a handful of powdery cement. The line of light below the door is now irregular. I crouch down and press my cheek against the floor. With one eye, I peer out. I see a patch of grass etched in moonlight.

My breath quickens. I use my nails and scratch again at the cement. It chips away and beneath it I smell fresh earth. Bless the decay that eats at concrete. My heart starts to race. I dig faster. Clumps of earth and cement crumble beneath my fingers. The silver particles that had been cast into the cement burn in my throat and sting my eyes, but it's not enough to stop me.

I dig. I cough. I dig. I cough. I dig.

The hole widens beneath the door. Just a little larger …

There is a tree root in the way. It's ironbark, too strong for me to break, but I can move it. Then I slip through. I stand upright. I let out a shuddering breath.

I am free.

It's midnight and the bush is quiet around me. Behind me, the ironbark tree that has imprisoned me for the last thousand years creaks loudly. It's calling to the pixies, letting them know I am free.

I turn and spit at it. My saliva sizzles as it hits the hidden door sealing the prison from this side. My gaolers artfully forged the surface to resemble the tree's rugged bark cloak. They don't want anyone finding me, and no one ever has.

A breeze stirs and parts the leaves overhead. A sliver of night sky is revealed. With it comes the moon. I tremble as her light glides over me. The human part of me recognises what is about to happen and wants me to run away, but I know it's too late. The wolf is already awakening.

Pain replaces my fear as I begin to change. My muscles lengthen, my skin sprouts hair; my fingernails sharpen into claws, a white hot, irrational rage rises up inside of me ...

I hear the music again. I fall to my haunches. The pixies are close by. They will want to put me back in the tree. But that is not an option.

I look up at the moon and howl to her, the goddess whom we werewolves worship. She responds, strengthening me, fortifying me. I roll my shoulders, testing my muscles; they are powerful now. I stretch my jaw. I feel my teeth extending.

I am ready.

And here they come, the pixies. Their devilish faces leer at me.

* * *

He's been scratching at the door for a thousand years. When the moon is new, he takes human form and is a gentle creature. But when the moon waxes full, he transforms into savagery incarnate. He becomes an animal, immortal, unable to be killed. So we imprisoned him in the tree long ago to protect the natural world. We pixies had felt regret for the fate of the man in him, but the sacrifice was deemed acceptable. The animal needed to be contained.

But now that animal is free, and on this night of all nights—the night of the blue moon; the only night the moon can lend her strength to him two-fold.

I twist and turn, my wings clipping at the edges of tree branches and leaves in my haste. The ironbark tree has called out its warning and we are coming. My brethren flit beside me, their beating wingtips trailing golden strains of pixie music in their wake. They are prepared to do what must be done.

We know the beast will not give up his freedom without a fight. But we cannot fail.

I fly beneath a fallen branch, over an anthill and into the clearing. The clouds and moon overhead paint a scene of patchwork silver and grey. I see him crouching, a black shadow cast against the moonlit grass. His dark muzzle raises, a long drawn-out howl pierces the night. He calls to his mistress, the moon. I peel back my lips into a grimace, praying her attention is elsewhere this night.

I zip forward, my wings clicking against each other as I increase speed. The air flows over and around me and then I am within the creature's reach.

He is covered in grey fur, and his teeth glitter, a row of yellow points in his jaw. Long, clawed fingers rake towards me, trying to tear me from the sky. I cartwheel in mid-flight, too fast for his clumsy attempt. I glance left. The others have the chain ready. It is a fine thing, a thread of pixie-wrought silver the consistency of spider silk. But it is strong.

My friends fly upwards in circles, dragging the chain with them. It bellows out in growing rings, clinging to the air like a string of dewdrops.

I need to keep the beast busy so the others can encircle him. I fly at his eyes and he grabs at me again. I bite at his fingers, rewarded with a half cry, half yelp of pain. The chain floats down around him, the edges of it guided by my pixie warriors. I tease him again. It will be over soon.

The yelp of pain as the first strand of the chain touches him almost drops me from the sky. I correct my course and join the others in the effort to pull the chain taut. The air soon stinks of charred fur and skin. The beast cries out in pain again. I wish there were a gentler way to detain him.

Suddenly, the moon is gone, blocked by the slowly moving clouds overhead.

The cries of the werewolf change. They are now the sobs of a man. He is naked, lying like a crumpled thing on the grass. The chain no longer scalds him, but it holds him fast. He cannot escape.

I alight on the ground near his head. My hand is only the size of his fingertip, but I use it to brush aside a strand of his dirty grey hair. His eyes open and he looks at me. They are a clear green and filled with tears. I thought I had forgotten those eyes, but the sting of my own tears pricking at the back of my eyelids tells me otherwise.

'It's been a long time,' I manage to say.

He smiles through his tears. 'Too long, my love.'

'You know what I must do, David.'

He sobs. 'Yes. I remember everything now.' He pauses, gulping down emotion too raw to comfortably witness. 'And I will forgive you for it, just as I have before.'

I lean over and kiss his brow, the brow of the man I once loved before the witch of the hill found us together on her land and changed him into a werewolf and me into a pixie. And even though I have had my revenge on that score—binding the witch to the ground beneath the hill—the reality remains the same.

I am a pixie warrior, a defender of the natural world, a being without the capacity to feel love. And he is a beast of folklore, an abomination to the natural world and one who, when in his wolf form, cannot recognise love.

In making us natural enemies, the witch tore us apart irrevocably.

I look back at him. 'Time to go.'

He nods. My brethren gather around and with many tiny hands lift him from the soft grass. As they carry him to the tree, he turns his face to the sky, as if looking for the moon that has abandoned him. But she remains hidden behind her shrouds of cloud.

I touch the door hidden in the tree. Purple lines of light course from my fingers and into the metal like blood through arteries. The door springs open on silent hinges. I look within the cavity and see the broken floor where he had dug himself free. I wave my hand across the hole and the cement transforms into a solid slab of stone traced through with veins of silver. He won't escape again.

My werewolf man is placed back into his prison. I see the resignation in his eyes and find myself afflicted with a sense of guilt. It surprises me. Pixies do not have emotions. Perhaps it is proof that there is actually some part of me that remains human.

I want to do something for him. I think for a moment and then wave my hand again. A small window appears in the forged prison door, disguised as a knothole. It is a small thing, but it will at least let him see out. I glide forward to help the others remove the bonds. He does not struggle.

Once done, the door to his prison is closed and sealed again.

I flit back as the moon breaks clear overhead. I wait for the savage response from the werewolf locked in the tree. But again I am surprised. Instead of howling, there is silence. I see a clear green eye pressed to the knothole, its gaze firmly fixed skyward. The werewolf is bound back to the tree, but he seems content as long as he can see the moon.

I think on the night as I wing my way home. Tonight a werewolf was calmed by a pixie afflicted with human emotion, an unusual state of affairs. I begin to question fate. Perhaps changing the spell cast by the witch beneath the hill is a possibility. Perhaps it has something to do with a blue moon.

I speed up. The music trailing from my wingtips changes tempo. Perhaps there is hope that I can regain the human life stolen from me. If so, against my faerie nature I intend to act upon it.

Just maybe I can release the man I once loved.

The Southern Cross

The land was flat, and the earth stained red by the light of a fading sunset. Jack let Warpaint have his head. The old Appaloosa stallion picked his way carefully through the tussocks of dried grass and towering red anthills that dotted the sparse landscape. Occasionally, his shod hooves would clank against an ancient granite boulder. The lizards lying on these rocks, soaking in the last heat of the day, skittered away at the sound; clawed feet kicking up dust in their wake.

Jack shaded his eyes against the fiery horizon. There was no chance of finding Harrison's lost cattle today. He was painfully short on water, and he needed to find the billabong.

He lowered his hand, watching as the last rays of sunlight fell from view. He smiled, feeling melancholy. As a drover he'd seen many a sunset in outback Australia, and it had always seemed to him that the sun paused in that last moment at the horizon line, as if it were hesitant to relinquish the land. He let his smile fade, wondering what it was that a sun could possibly fear.

The afternoon had surrendered to twilight before the billabong came into view. Jack let out a breath. The spindly trees and reeded banks sure were a welcome sight. Warpaint's ears flitted forward and a tired nicker escaped his lips.

Jack leaned over affectionately to slap the horse's neck. 'That's right, mate, fresh water and a place for supper.'

Warpaint needed no further encouragement. He broke into a weary trot.

Jack tried to ignore the stiffness he sensed in the old horse's gait. Age was catching up with the stallion, but Jack hadn't the heart to put him out to pasture just yet. He smiled. The other blokes were always saying he should take on a stockhorse; better for droving than a worn-out Appaloosa, they said. But Warpaint had heart, and while the horse was happy to keep droving, Jack wouldn't stop him.

The billabong, with its half-submerged trees, seemed almost ethereal in the dusk, a place that existed somewhere between reality and dreams. The dark water, cocooned in the shallow depression of land, was still, a mirrored disk reflecting back upon itself the blushed copper sky. Native lily pads lazed like tiny rafts on the surface, pond skaters flitting between them in search of their evening meal.

Jack slithered off Warpaint's back, his boots thudding quietly as they hit the sun-baked bank. He reached up and unbuckled the empty canteen from his saddle. Warpaint ambled down ahead of him to the water's edge and dropped his muzzle to drink. But instead of sinking his nose into the cool water, the horse raised it quickly, snorting air loudly through quivering nostrils.

Jack walked down. 'What is it?' His nose wrinkled. Something dead was close by.

Following the line of the bank, his gaze fell on the bloated carcass of a brown-and-white bullock lying in the water. He picked his way over to the corpse. Even in the dim light, the brand was clearly visible on the animal's haunch. It was one of Harrison's, all right.

'Dammit!' snarled Jack, knowing the old man would take the cost of the animal out of his wage.

Jack held the sleeve of his shirt over his nose and grabbed one of the back legs. The hide was slimy, and the rancid meat clinging to the bone sponge-like. He shuddered. Straining, he pulled the carcass clear of the water and dropped it on the bank. He flicked his fingers in disgust. The stink was even more powerful now.

Jack glanced over at Warpaint, who was none too impressed either. His ears were laid back and his nostrils flared wide.

Jack sighed. The dead animal caused him more problems than one. The carcass, rotting in the heat like that, would have tainted the water. And with the station still five days' ride away, and this being the only waterhole between here and there ... well, he and Warpaint would be hard-pressed to make it back alive.

Jack reached down, grabbed a handful of sand and rubbed his palms together to remove the smell. He made his way back to Warpaint and ran a hand down the stallion's nose. Warpaint nickered, the sound a query.

Jack looked into the horse's warm brown eye. 'Sorry, mate, no water tonight.'

* * *

The night was dark, and overhead the stars were a threaded patchwork of silver. Jack settled back into his swag. He wasn't sure what he was going to do, but decided it was tomorrow's problem to solve. Long habit saw his gaze swing upward, searching for the Southern Cross. It was there, high above him, blazing like a jewelled necklace in the velvet sky. He smiled to himself. Everything would work out. In other scrapes, those stars had always led him home.

The breeze picked up from out of the night, and Warpaint, tethered to a nearby tree, shuffled nervously as the scent of the dead animal coiled around them again.

'Settle down,' said Jack. 'That bullocks past causin' us any bother beyond his stink.'

Warpaint huffed.

Jack chuckled. 'You shouldn't be scared of ghosts at your age.' He clutched his blanket closer to his shoulder and rolled over to settle in for the night. As he did, a glow beyond the trees caught his attention.

He sat up. Uneasy, he reached for the rifle lying by his side.

The glow circled behind the bank of the billabong, casting an eerie shimmer across the water. A chill ran up Jack's spine. He suddenly felt as if facing whatever this was would be better done on his feet. He picked up the rifle and went to stand by Warpaint.

'Easy,' he whispered, placing his hand on the horse's wither. The stallion was trembling.

The light, shaped like a disc, emerged silently from behind an old twisted log. Jack tightened his grip on the rifle. He'd heard enough stories. He knew what it was.

The Min Min light stopped a few feet away, its glow illuminating the ground beneath it. It hovered, as if considering the man and horse.

Jack put the rifle to his shoulder. His trembling finger instinctively fell to the trigger. 'What do you want?' he yelled out.

The light moved closer.

Warpaint reared, his neigh a shrill scream as he tore free of the tether. Jack fell backwards. With the gun still clutched in one hand, the other rose in defence. Poor armour against a horse's flailing hooves, but somehow Warpaint avoided him. Jack cowered on the ground and watched the stallion strike at the disc.

Hoof met light.

Light flared.

Warpaint disappeared.

'No!'

Jack struggled to his feet, desperate to find his friend. He stumbled, disorientated by the flash of light that had ruined his night vision. He blinked rapidly and gradually his eyesight cleared. The light had moved, but still hovered a short distance away. Of Warpaint, there was no sign.

Never having felt so scared in his life, Jack lifted the rifle again, aimed and squeezed the trigger.

Jack kept firing until the chamber clicked empty, each bullet striking the disc of light and disintegrating in a scattering of tiny sparks. He threw the gun aside and reached for the only weapon he had left, his skinning knife. He pulled the thin blade free from his belt.

'Come and get me, then,' he snarled.

The Min Min, as if awaiting the invitation, moved forward.

Jack grimaced, baring his teeth like a dingo. He shuffled the knife in his grip. A line of cold fire blazed down its length. This was it.

Time slowed as the light approached. Jack thought he could see things moving within the glowing disc. Formless shadows. Curiosity diminished his fear. He leaned in closer to look. The shadows slowly morphed into an image of a dark sky ornamented by a cluster of burning stars: the Southern Cross.

'Will you follow the stars?' The words were a whisper, spoken by the light.

Jack felt as if he were caught in a dream. 'Yes. Follow the stars.'

He reached for the disc. Light engulfed him.

He was clinging to the back of an old Appaloosa stallion. Warpaint. The horse was in full flight, reins flying free as he galloped with fierce determination through the shadowed landscape. Jack grasped desperately at the reins. He caught them and huddled low over Warpaint's wither to match the horse's rhythm.

Before long, other lights emerged in the near distance. Station lights? No. Not the warm lights of home, but a small cluster of cold, pale spheres. A seed of dread lodged in Jack's stomach, but with no other landmark to head for, he guided Warpaint toward them.

As they approached, the lights changed shape. Jack felt his heart skip a beat. They were not spheres at all, but the ghostly outlines of twelve cattle—the remainder of Harrison's lost herd.

Jack pulled Warpaint to a halt. Around them, the spirit animals stood watching expectantly.

Jack felt his legs begin to tremble. To steady himself, he placed a hand on Warpaint's mane. The stallion swung his head around to look back. It was not a warm brown eye that locked onto Jack's, but a pale orb filled with cold light.

Jack screamed. He threw himself from the stallion's back. As he fell, he went to use his hands to break the fall, but saw that they were no longer hands. He screamed again, louder this time.

Where warm flesh had once existed, now there was only pale, cold light.

Light that outlined, in silver, the shape and edges of the man he had been.

Soldier Angel

The intersection is full of people; bustling professionals on their way to work, three buskers playing guitars on a threadbare blanket, a group of primary schoolers, their teacher. And me.

There is also a crumpled newspaper.

It's lying on the footpath where a businessman in a dark blue pinstripe suit dropped it. I pick it up and smooth the front page. A face appears out of the folds: an Australian soldier, the latest to have died in Afghanistan. He was a sapper, it says, killed by an improvised explosive device. He was only young, twenty-three years.

I look away. A family will be crying somewhere for him tonight.

I watch the tide of people sweep by me. I wonder if any give a thought to the fallen soldier. A thought to how he died, or what sacrifices he made for their freedom. Probably not, but I know that to expect more from civilians is futile. They don't have the experience necessary to understand what we endure when sent to those faraway, war-torn places. They don't get that it's more than just a physical displacement; there is the mental ruin of us also.

But in saying that, I consider myself better off than most. Unlike a few of the other guys, I no longer have the desire to end it all. My focus is now on my future. I'm looking forward to going home.

It's been a year since my wife Lara had me admitted to the military psychiatric hospital. I don't regret her sending me there. She saved my life by doing it. I'm not proud to admit that I had a breakdown, but the thought of going back over there had undone me. It would have been my third tour in Afghanistan. And the voice in my head was insistent: *Don't go. Don't go. Don't go.*

Well, that day ended with me trying to commit suicide. Death by an alcoholic cocktail mixed with Valium might seem like a coward's way out, but it was a clean option. A bullet in the head is messy and not something I wanted my family to see.

Lara found me unconscious that night and the paramedics she called pulled me back from the brink. Since then, my time at the facility has changed my outlook. I'm ready now to rejoin society.

The newspaper slides through my fingers as I let it fall back to the footpath. I look around me, taking in the bustle and beauty of the morning. The sunlight filtering down between the buildings is warm and the jumbled city sounds are a quiet roar as I wait on the corner. I keep a lookout for Lara. She's on her way to pick me up.

My two teenage daughters will be waiting for me at home. I fear what I will read in their eyes when I see them. Will it be disgust with the father who failed to kill himself? Or pride for the soldier who has since then worked hard to battle his demons? My wife tells me they understand, but still, my anticipation at seeing them wars with my apprehension.

But for now, I need to stay focused. I take a deep breath to calm my anxiety. I'm rewarded with the distracting aroma of roasting coffee. The smell is coming from the coffee cart on the corner. It's been a long time since I had a good coffee and the thought of it makes my mouth water.

I dig into my pocket and fish out the five-dollar note I know is crumpled at the bottom. I pick up my pack and move to stand in the coffee line. There are two people ahead of me.

An older woman is dressed in a black jacket, skirt and heels. Her white hair is styled into a chic bob. I imagine her to be an interior designer as she orders her chai latte—soy, no sugar—in a regular cup.

Behind her is a much larger man. His shirt is dark brown and, even though it is early, already sweat marks mar the armpits. His belly sags over his belt like a badly folded bivvy bag as he taps away with short, stubby fingers on his smartphone. To me he seems like an accountant, a man who sits alone behind a worn desk in a plain room. One who is good with figures and has an addiction to takeaway lunches.

The woman finishes placing her order and moves off to one side.

Mr Accountant shuffles forward and orders. 'A long black. Double shot. No sugar, thanks.'

The coffee vendor looks up at him. I notice he's sweating, too. The moisture glistens on his brow. He is a slim man, with mocha-coloured skin and green eyes. European, maybe. He doesn't reply to Mr Accountant, doesn't even smile. He just nods as he reaches over for a takeaway cup.

There is something about the barista that makes me feel uncomfortable. He looks uneasy as he steams the milk for Ms

Interior Designer's latte. It's as if his hands are not familiar with the task. I watch as he reaches for the powdered cocoa container; watch as his hands tremble while sprinkling the chocolate over the frothed milk.

He seems anxious.

I think he's biding his time, waiting for something.

He hands Ms Interior Designer her chai latte and she walks off. Mr Accountant shuffles to the side to wait for his. I move up, locking eyes with the barista as I do. This close, I can see that the man's eyes are bloodshot. Suddenly he looks away from me, as if he recognises something in me that he's not entirely comfortable with either.

'What would you like?' he asks in an accented voice. His origin is hard to place.

'Cappuccino, thanks.'

The man nods and reaches down to open the small fridge below the coffee machine. As he leans over, his shirtfront falls open. I see trailing lines of wires running across his chest, the line of a vest below it. He stands back up and catches me staring. His face darkens; his mouth goes flat.

At the same time, I feel a hand on my shoulder. I turn. It's Lara. She's smiling, a vision with her long dark hair swept back over her shoulder.

'Hi, love,' she says. 'Order me a latte, too?'

Shit.

The world contracts around me. I swing back to look at the barista. He fumbles in his shirt, his hand emerging holding a trigger-switch. Mr Accountant sees it at the same time I do and swears. He turns to run, screaming *Bomb!* as he goes.

Chaos erupts. People scream. The barista is babbling a prayer, his eyes wild.

There is no time for words. No time to run. I push my wife to the ground. I reach instinctively for a weapon that I don't have. I lock eyes with the barista.

There is light; there is heat, and then darkness.

* * *

I am suspended in a void. Above me stretches a black ocean dotted with pinpoints of light. Stars. There's no sound and I'm neither warm nor cold. I'm alone, but if I strain my senses I think I can hear music, faint like chiming bells. But no, it's not bells. It's something else. Voices, I think. They sound like angels.

One of the stars begins to move towards me. Its white light changes; it turns gold as it approaches. When its size matches my own, it begins to morph. Two long graceful scythes emerge from the top of it, fluid, as the intricate detail is resolved into two brilliant white wings, feathered and scattered with golden scales. An impossibly beautiful face, its eyes closed, takes form. Pale blond hair, glistening like corn silk, falls across a steep forehead. Two muscled arms emerge crossed over a naked male chest of marble-white skin. Legs, waist and leather battle skirt manifest and solidify.

Then he exists, in all his brightness and gleaming glory.

His eyes open. The pupils are slitted, and the irises coloured gold and orange. They are eyes that belong in the face of a demon, not an angel like I suspect him to be.

'Name: William Lorn.' The angel's lips do not move as he speaks, and my name sounds more of a statement than a greeting. He continues, listing facts. 'Born: twelfth of August 1976. Religion: Catholic. Occupation: Australian Army sergeant, 2nd Commando Regiment. Kills: ten. Lives saved: five hundred. Status: dead. Balance weighed: entry into heaven permitted.'

The angel stops. His slitted eyes drop away from mine and his head tilts to one side as if he is listening. The sound of angelic voices swells louder around me. The angel's eyes return to mine. They are filled with pity. He speaks again.

'Year 2010: attempted suicide. Balance adjusted: entry into heaven denied.'

'What the hell are you talking about?' I ask, ignoring the creeping chill that travels up my spine.

'Suicide is a mortal sin,' replies the angel.

The cold in my spine travels up to my chest. 'Sin? But I'm not dead. I survived. I chose a new path. Please. I just want to go home.'

The angel tilts his head at me. His otherworldly eyes glitter. 'But you have passed, William. You cannot go home.'

His words hit me like a punch to the belly. I suddenly remember the intersection, the coffee cart, Mr Accountant and Ms Interior Designer. The barista. My wife. My anxiety suddenly peaks.

'My wife, where is she?' I look around, desperate. But I see nothing except the vast black void with its canopy of stars stretching into the distance.

The angel speaks again, his voice intoning facts. 'Name: Lara Lorn. Born: sixteenth October 1980. Status: living. Condition: critical.'

'She's alive?'

'Yes.'

'I need to get to her. I need to get home. My girls—'

'You cannot return home. You are headed elsewhere.'

Suddenly I'm angry. I want to strike out at the angel, hurt him. 'What do you mean elsewhere? Hell? Too late for that, already been there and back. Have lived with the scars of it for a long time now.' I fling my words like venom. I spew them out all over his brightness.

The angel does not flinch. Instead he leans in closer. 'Your sin aside, you were a good man, William. A good soldier who saved more than you killed. And yes, I can send you to hell and it would be far worse than you have yet endured, but first I'll ask you to consider my alternative.'

Alternative? What alternative? I want to ask the question, but I'm too angry. I think he sees this. His face is solemn as he reaches over to grasp my shoulder. His touch is like fire but with it comes clarity. It's like the opening of a window into the angel's own soul.

I suddenly know him to be the Archangel Michael and I see that he understands me completely. For myself, I recognise him as the soldier he is, a soldier just like me. And even if it was a mortal sin, I know that he understands my attempt to end my life, for he too has suffered loss and witnessed atrocities. And now he's asking me to join him. Asking me to take my wounded soul and use the good left in it to fight by his side.

But do I want to be a soldier angel for God?

I feel tears prick the back of my eyes. Yes. There is something appealing to me about having died only to rise up and fight again for a righteous cause. But there is one thing left to do.

'Can I see them one last time?' I ask.

Michael lets go of my shoulder and stands upright again. He waves his hand, and beneath it the starry backdrop of the void wrinkles. A window forms suspended in the space between us. It looks into a hospital room.

My wife is lying awake in the bed; her face is scratched and her hair burnt away, but she still looks beautiful to me. My two daughters sit by her side; they look just like their mother, just as beautiful. Their eyes, full of tears, are fixed to a television screen mounted to the far wall.

The news is on, headlines run along the bottom of the screen. One catches my attention.

Local Afghanistan war veteran William Lorn dies with 26 others in street-side terrorist attack.

I look back at my family. I want so much to gather them into my arms and tell them it will all be okay. But there is only one thing left to say.

'Goodbye,' I whisper.

My wife and daughters turn as one as if to look at me, tears glistening on their cheeks. I reach out to them, but as I touch the window, it ripples beneath my fingertips and fades. I fall to my knees, clutching my grief to my chest. I weep silently for the things I've done to my family and those left undone.

A hand touches my shoulder. 'Their healing will start with your goodbye,' says Michael.

'Yes,' I reply. 'But for me, the image of them grieving will last an eternity.'

'I know.' The angel's tone is grim. 'But that's a burden all soldier angels bear.'

I lower my chin to my chest. My tears continue to fall, matching those of the family crying somewhere for me tonight.

This Wild Stretch of Ocean

In the late season of that year, we were living in a fishing boat on a wild stretch of ocean. Each day saw the endless vistas of water and sky painted differently. One day would be an impressionist's study of pale blues, a wash of colour that blurred the horizon. The next would be a tempest of waves, their rough, stroked tips tinged red as they battered against a fierce sunset.

But always, no matter how the sea looked, the men in my employ worked hard. Every day I heard their voices bellowing out loudly to combat the song of the ocean—that symphony of natural music that was a blend of raucous seagull song, the shriek of the wind through cables, and the splash of waves against the *Matilda's* metal hull. Such are the normal sounds of a fisherman's life; such were the sounds that saw us to our misadventure.

It was a day when the sky was grey and the wind blustered cold. The ocean was coloured graphite, her temperament mean as she arched and swelled her back in agitated motion. Even the

PAMELA JEFFS

seagulls sat quietly along the *Matilda*'s rail; their bright orange beaks huddled deep into their ruffled white chests.

Hans, the first mate, entered the wheelhouse, a blast of frigid air following him. 'It's turning evil outside, Robert,' he said.

I ran my fingers through my beard, pausing for a moment to scratch at the dimple beneath my chin. 'Right-o. Call the boys in for supper.'

He nodded and headed back through the door. I heard his voice bellowing out the command and the grateful cheers of the men on deck. They would soon be gathered in the galley, taking the chance to warm their frigid fingers before I sent them back out on deck to reset the longlines.

I envied them their moment of respite. I had been at the wheel for twenty-four hours straight and it would be another ten before I could take the time to rest. This stretch of ocean was one where I didn't trust the sailing to anyone else, a stretch of sea that was as treacherous as it was beautiful. There were other places for us to fish, but coming here meant a quick catch that would see the men home to Narooma for Christmas. Not something other captains cared about, but such considerations were what kept these good men loyal to my *Matilda*.

I settled back into my seat, the worn leather giving way to my bulk with a quiet shush of sound. My eyes stung. I reached for the chipped coffee cup on the timber shelf above the throttle. Fifteen years of use had left the timber permanently stained with coffee rings. I took a swig and grimaced. The coffee was not only bitter but also stone cold. I drank it anyway, anything to stave off the need for sleep.

106

I almost missed the flash of blue that sparked on the horizon. I was awake in an instant. The short flare blazed out again, bright against the dull surface of the ocean. I sat forward in my chair, brushing at the haze gathered on the inside of the cabin windows.

I saw the flash again, closer this time. And then again. Suddenly it was riding alongside *Matilda*'s bow wave, a pale form beneath the water. It broke the surface and then I saw her: an impossible reality.

Her hair was long and coloured white. Eyes, greener than emeralds, held me in thrall. The line of her neck and the mounds of her breasts were scaled silver, the tracery leading down to meet with a tail, metallic blue in colour. I stared at the fins that flared at its base; they were long and ephemeral, streaming behind her in the current.

She neither smiled nor waved, but returned my stare with a solemn regard. *Such terrible mistakes you have made*, her eyes seemed to say.

She lifted her left hand clear of the water. In it she held the corpse of a Bluefin tuna. Its streamlined metallic body was dulled in death, the thin, grey skin tarnished with the whip-like marks left from a longline wrapping around its once living, struggling body.

Then I understood. This was the mermaid's ocean, and our catch were her charges to protect.

Suddenly, around me the familiar sounds of the sea fell silent and the storm-coloured daylight faded. In the glare of our deck lights, I could see the gulls still huddled on the rail, but instead of looking out over water, they now stared into complete and utter darkness. I could hear the quiet throbbing of *Matilda*'s engines.

I reached over and opened the cabin's side window. I had to push hard to make the salt-frosted glass run along its corroded track. It moved, but the shriek of sound it made jarred painfully in my ears. I pushed my face through the opening and took a deep breath.

The air outside smelt like pitch.

Voices, deep and filled with concern, floated up the staircase leading from the galley. The words were crowded as they jostled against each other in the tight space. I glanced across at the hatch just as Hans emerged from it, his solid bulk leading the pack of sailors that followed.

'What's happened?' he asked.

Hans, normally unshakable by nature, sounded afraid. I could hear the fear in his voice; see the lines of worry etched on his face. As captain it was my job to reassure him, but I found, for the first time ever, that I could not.

'Not sure.' I hesitated, debating whether to tell them the truth. I decided that nothing was to be gained by omission. 'I saw a mermaid off our bow. I think she took us.'

Mutters rose from the men. Bad luck it was to see a mermaid. Worse luck if she saw fit to take you.

I pulled back on the throttle and *Matilda*'s motors shivered into silence. I pushed myself up from the seat and pulled the peak of my baseball cap down over my forehead. 'Let's go take a look.'

The air on deck was still and humid. The smell of pitch was stronger here. I sniffed, ignoring the burn of it in the back of my throat. The men fanned out behind me, some of them holding the sleeves of their yellow all-weather jackets pressed to their noses. I imagined the rubber fabric would do little to help.

Matilda's white rail was a ghostly shadow against the darkness. The gulls shuffled sideways as I approached, seemingly loathe to leave the only visible resting place.

I leaned over the rail and looked down. We were floating on a sea of motionless tar. Thick and greasy, the liquid clung to *Matilda*'s sides like black ink. Then it began to move. Sluggishly at first, then it started to pulse as if imbued with life. In horror, I watched as fingers of the stuff started to crawl up the sides of the boat. *Matilda* groaned.

The men started to curse softly as we listed gently to the port side. I glanced back at them. Their faces were as white as the rail.

'Get your suits on,' I ordered. They were only too keen to comply, jumping into frantic action before the words were out.

All-weather jackets were stripped off as Hans handed out the orange survival suits. One was thrust into my own hand and I ripped off my hat before feeding my booted feet into it. The fabric was pliant and comforting.

Around us *Matilda* groaned again. Her voice was an eerie sigh that cut softly through the darkness. Next to me, the gulls responded. Their white wings, shaped like scythes, opened as they left their perches on the rail. I watched them fly out across the tar ocean, their pale outlines visible momentarily against the oily surface below. Then without warning the birds burst into smoke, leaving trailers of the stuff floating downwards to meet with the sea. One moment they had been there and the next they were gone.

I looked back at the men, hoping they had missed seeing the gulls' fate, but it was too late. They had seen and now they feared for their own lives. All hell broke loose.

'Stand fast!' I yelled as they scrabbled across the deck towards the rope hold. They stopped, their eyes wide as they stared back at me expectantly.

'We need to secure ourselves,' said Hans.

'Let's be orderly about it then,' I said.

Matilda was listing dangerously now. I grasped the rail to steady my steps as I made my way across the deck. Fingers of tar had now reached the upper planks and the footing was treacherous. I unzipped the front of my suit and pulled my hands free. The door to the hold swung open easily. Inside, coils of rope were stacked neatly for easy retrieval. I pulled one out, the nylon threads coarse against my bare skin.

I handed it to Hans, who uncoiled the length and began to tie the rope around the hips of the men. He had only just managed to secure himself to me when the *Matilda* slid out from beneath us.

We had neglected to tie off the other end of the rope.

The shock as the tar slid over my head was like ice. With the deck lights gone, we were consumed by the utter darkness. I fought, trying to reach the surface, at the same time feeling the struggles of the others strung out along the rope.

My head broke free and I sucked in an urgent breath. Fluid ran down my face into my mouth and I tasted salt. Surprised, I realised the ocean was not tar at all, but good, honest saltwater.

I blinked my eyes clear. Bobbing in place, I looked around me. For a moment there was only the darkness, and the sound of grunting and gasping as my men struggled to get their breath. Then the horizon lightened as a blue sun rose slowly over the water, burnishing it to sapphire.

We were strung out across the water, tied to the rope like a string of tuna on a longline. A quiet splash drew my attention. I turned. Before me, floating like a jewelled queen was the mermaid.

She smiled at me this time, her small teeth strung like perfect pearls against her shell-pink lips. Her thought fluttered unspoken between us: *A fitting end*, she seemed to say.

But I had other ideas.

The Ghost and
the Immortal

Water, blood, fire and fear; the morning is drenched with them. But I move unaffected. Experience breeds apathy, and with this day years in the making, the constant reliving of my past has left me feeling so tired. I wish I could end it, but I am driven; always the curse compels.

The deck of my ship, the merchant vessel *Australis*, is a rolling causeway of hell. The sea priest's blessing, given to supposedly protect against the 'ill luck' of my female captaincy, does nothing to soften *Australis*'s passage through the channel now. The ship groans like a pregnant animal under the lash of storm-driven waves. Loose coils of waxed rope lie tangled underfoot and unfettered gunpowder barrels shunt against my shins. Splintered lengths of the shattered mast career across the salt-slippery deck.

'Watch out, Captain, ma'am!' I hear Michelson cry.

As I have a thousand times before, I dodge sideways and watch a piece of the mast fly by me. I know what I will see even before I look back: the splinter of timber is lodged in Michelson's chest. I lock eyes with him. I see his shock, and watch him fall limp to the deck. A wave carries him overboard in a tumble of blood-tinged water and sea foam.

The fire in the belly of the ship has broken through to the deck, fed by my precious whiskey barrels stowed in the hold. Billowing coils of black smoke that shift across the deck are thick with the smell. Shadows battle through the mess; the pale outlines of my sailors looking like puppets jerking on strings.

The fighting is fiercest by the bow. I head toward it, stumbling over a loose cannonball as I do. Then I see it. The flicker of a red leather vest appearing out of the smoke—a flash point glimpse of him, wild eyed, fighting like a great cat.

Jeremy Jones. Plunderer. Pirate. Murderer.

My brother.

He stands alone atop the bowsprit with the bodies of my sailors stacked below him. His sword drips blood, his fierce smile is all teeth and elation. The sight of him makes the curse in my blood flare; a searing flood of hate that is not my own.

Against my will, I pull my pistol clear of its holster.

I brace myself and aim.

I fire.

But the ship rolls awkwardly. My foot slips and my shot flies wide. I fall hard to the deck and am sent sliding down the blood-soaked length. I end up below the bowsprit, halted by the pile of bodies. The deck timbers smell like salt and blood. I look up. My brother stands above me. Then the ship rolls again and he stumbles. Falling from his perch, he lands sprawled across me.

Pain blossoms across my abdomen. I sob. My grip tightens on Jeremy's arm.

His sword is buried point first in my belly.

Jeremy's face sags, all joy wiped away. 'No! No, Morgan!' he whispers.

But it's too late. My blood, a captain's blood, is on the blessed timbers of *Australis*'s deck. And the law of the sea is exacting; the blood of the innocent shall always be avenged.

I hear the rising pitch of the wind, the sudden, strident roar of the waves. Beneath us, the sea gods begin to stir.

A king wave rushes the deck, and Jeremy and I are pulled from the ship. My grip slips off his arm as the water sucks me down. I glimpse *Australis*'s hull as it rides over me. Then my brother's ship, the *Raider*, follows her. In the water around me, I see other sailors struggling to reach the surface. The already dead just hang limply.

Deeper, in the darkness below, shapes begin to manifest. An emerald eye, the size of a ship; a mountainous elbow; a hand reaching, fingers the size of whales …

The sea god's touch is like fire against my skin. His ancient magic begins to flow through me, the bitter sting of my curse renewed. I fall limp in his grasp. All I know is pain; all is the fire of his self-righteous anger.

'Take my power, take my rage,' he whispers, 'Avenge yourself.'

Then there is darkness.

* * *

Noon. My arms are entangled in rope and draped over a timber barrel. The storm has passed, having given way to a bright sky and calm seas. My wound is a sharp ache in my stomach. Or is it the fire of the sea god's curse? All I know is that it hurts. I press my palm against it, but find little surcease. I close my eyes and rest my cheek back against the barrel. I let the currents carry me.

* * *

The sound of sand scraping against the barrel wakens me. Land. I open my eyes, but at first my vision is blurry. A crust of dried salt clings to my eyelashes; the tiny crystals sharp edged and painful. My body aches and my belly feels hot. I untangle myself from the ropes and crawl up the beach. I rest in the shade of the cliffs to wait for nightfall.

* * *

It's close to midnight. I dread what I know is coming. I try to remain still, to refuse the compulsion that drives me, but the curse is a cruel master. It forces me to my feet. I head for the waterline.

Jeremy is always somewhere along the southern line of coast. I follow the familiar path to the place where the cliffs meet the water. The stone is slippery there and rugged, but with the tide out, the trek can be made. I am wet, and my wound has started to seep blood again by the time I clear the last outcrop of stone.

Beyond is a small cliff-lined bay. Its white sand is rimed silver with moonlight, and the rocky walls shudder and shift in the glow of a small fire. My steps slow, my heart beats faster. I don't want to be here, I don't want to do this.

I love my brother.

Jeremy slumbers, curled on the sand between his fire and the cliffs. The line of his broad shoulder; the curve of his well-muscled back faces me. He sleeps on his rolled-up red leather vest.

The next thing I know, I am standing over him, a thick club of driftwood gripped tightly in my fist. I hold it above his head. The god's rage is coursing through my veins. Words race through my mind. *Kill him. Avenge yourself. Spill his blood.*

I feel the hate swell even more. If only he hadn't tried to steal the whisky from me, if only he hadn't accidently stabbed me, if only … how different our fates would have been. It's his fault that I must dance this dance, his fault that I must kill him over and over.

His fault.

But deep down, past the magic of the curse, I know the truth. Not his fault at all.

But it doesn't matter. This night will end as it always ends. I will live. My brother will die. And then it will begin all over again.

Jeremy is awake. I see his black eyes open, two glittering mirrors of chipped glass. I see the fire dancing in them, two red points of colour. Then he is on his feet. His gaze slides over my weapon and then up.

'Is it time already?' Jeremy's voice is weary.

'Yes.'

His shoulders droop. He looks resigned. 'Then end it quickly.'

He looks as tired as I feel. I take in the lines of my brother's lean muscles as they catch the firelight, his dark, lank hair and, crusted with salt, his scarred body. The curse cannot stem the wash of guilt

I feel. Those scars tell the story of his terrible existence. I gave them to him. One for each night I have killed him. But the hate impregnated in my bones is at odds with my personal sentiments.

I lift the club. I swallow.

I am about to swing when the sound of beating wings stops me. A seagull, white and grey, lands on the beach between us. It fixes a pale eye upon me and I feel that eye raze me to the core. This bird is more than just a bird. I feel released when the bird's gaze moves to fix upon Jeremy.

The gull caws. *'Your sister loves you. Why do you punish her so?'*

Jeremy is punishing me?

'I'm punishing myself,' Jeremy says, his face hardening. 'I deserve it for what I did to her.'

The gull's voice is also hardened. *'Let the past go. Move forward.'*

There is power in those words. I feel their compulsion; they soften the drive of the curse. I am free enough to ask, 'Who are you?'

The bird looks at me. *'One who doesn't believe the sea gods wield absolute power. And one tired of witnessing your bloodshed.'*

My anger flares. The sea god whispers in my mind. *Will you let a bird judge you? Kill him.*

But then I see bird's eyes glow and somehow recognise its judgment to be fair. My anger abates. 'You are no gull.'

'No. And I am no friend of the sea gods either.'

Then, as I watch, the bird's eye seems to grow, and in it I glimpse a world of cloud and air: the domain of the air gods. I suddenly smell the scent of crisp, clean air, and with it, the curse ends. The world shifts around me, and my mind is clear for the first time in a century.

Then I see an old man sitting on the sand. He looks sad. 'I'm sorry, Morgan,' he says. 'So sorry.'

I drop my club and kneel by his side. 'Jeremy?' I reach over to touch the man's hair, hair I suspect was once black but is now iron grey. Then I know for sure. Yes, it is my brother. His skin has sagged with age, and deep lines crease his cheeks. But his scars … they remain unchanged.

'What's happening?' I ask, confused.

'I killed you. And then the sea gods cursed me for it. I could see the sister I love for eternity, but must bear death each day to do so.'

'I hated hurting you.'

'It was the only way I could pay for what I did.'

I look down at my belly. I rest a hand against my wound. 'So I'm dead?'

'Yes,' he whispers, the word carrying the weight of his grief.

I look over at the bird. 'Is my brother dead also?'

'No,' the gull says. *'He was rendered immortal. Never to end, never to find peace.'*

'Is that so?' I feel a different kind of rage begin to well up in me. I reach over and reclaim my club. I get to my feet.

My brother's eyes widen in shock. 'What are you doing?'

'Ending this.' I turn and face the ocean.

The gull caws, a raucous sound. *'A mere club will not serve you to that end.'*

'What else do I have?'

The gull tilts its head. *'You have me. Agree to fight and I'll defend your flank.'*

118

Jeremy rises and moves stiffly to take his place by my side. 'And you have me.'

I flash Jeremy a reassuring smile. The one he returns transcends time. It's the fierce grin of his youth, the grin I saw on his younger face when he was standing on *Australis*'s bowsprit. He suddenly doesn't look so worn.

'Together, little sister,' he says.

The gods must know we are waiting for them. My hair is whipped wild as the wind rises and waves begin to rush the beach. Out on the horizon, fingers the size of whales surge up out of the water.

They are coming, the sea gods.

And I find I am not afraid.

I am ready.

Waking Io

I see a man alone, in the middle of the desert. He looks to be half-starved and all crazy. But he doesn't have the telling scar. So, even crazy, he just might be worth saving.

I nudge Cleopatra, my mare, closer. I can feel in the sudden bunching of her muscles her hesitation to approach the man. And I can't blame her. The man looks strange, and it's not only that he's naked. There's something about his eyes, the colour of them. They're an unnatural blue, the exact shade of the far ocean I dream about every night.

But perhaps they seem bluer because his smooth, tanned skin is so dark and his hair is so white. It's not hair de-saturated by age, but white-blond, with its length crusted into dreadlocks that hang halfway down his back. Most strange of all, he is currently facing down a prickly pear.

'Which way to the ocean?' he screams at the plant.

I reply on behalf of the cactus. 'You're a long way from the ocean here, mate.'

The man starts. His eyes swing around and I see them take in the details of my horse, the whip on my saddle and my riding gear. His gaze slides up past my dusty jean-clad legs and over my faded red cotton-check shirt. He takes in my auburn braid, half hidden beneath my wide-brimmed hat.

'I'm named Io, not *mate*. Tell me where I am, woman.'

His strange accent makes the tone of his voice sound all the more dangerous. It feels weighted like a storm brewing behind a mountain range. I'm tempted to pull my whip free, but something holds me back.

'Lake Eyre, Australia,' I say. 'You're in the middle of the goddamn desert.'

He looks confused. Maybe it's sunstroke. 'Australia?' he whispers.

'Yeah. Australia.'

Io's hands, scarred and bloodied, as if he has used them to crawl his way across the continent, rise to cover his face. 'By the shifting tide … I'm not in my own time.'

Any further questions from me are met with silence.

* * *

It's night and we sit across from each other, an open fire glittering between us. He looks slightly better now he's clothed in my full-length oilskin jacket, but I sense that his mind is still hard and wild. And his fingers, they never rest. They pluck, almost of their own accord, at the ends of his hair, at the peeling skin on the backs of his hands.

I reach over and stir the stew in the pot I have simmering on coals next to the fire. The thick, rich scent of stewing rabbit and wild vegetables makes my mouth water. But as the smell wafts on the cool evening breeze, Io's nose wrinkles up in distaste.

'You don't like stew?' I ask, thinking that a starving man should be more grateful.

'What year is it?' he snaps at me suddenly. 'What gods are worshipped?'

So he's finally ready to talk, but about gods? The question is off kilter. Where has this man been for the last two hundred years? How could he not know? Even crazy, he should know. I keep my voice even.

'It's 2268,' I reply. 'And gods? There are no gods.'

He looks shocked. '2268?'

'Yes.'

'No gods?'

'No. No gods.'

His peculiar eyes track the landscape of my face as if trying to determine the truth there. 'Who are you and why are you out here?' He gestures toward the darkened landscape, 'Out in this ... desert?'

'My name's Sasha. And I'm a woman who searches.'

'For what?'

'For anyone left alive, of course.'

'Alive?' Io turns his attention to the moonlit darkness out beyond the camp. Cleopatra shifts just outside the line of firelight, one of her shod hooves clanking quietly against a rock. A log on the fire crackles. 'What's happened to the world?' he asks softly.

He doesn't seem to expect me to answer. And truthfully, I couldn't give one even if he did. All I know is that the world is dangerous for those who don't bear the scar. And there are only fifty other humans I know of who don't. Everyone else on the continent looks and moves like a human, but since the Change none of them are alive, not really.

Without living souls to sustain belief, faith has faltered. Not that I ever believed in gods to begin with. If you ask me, the stories were only ever fanciful tales told so the weak could understand the world. But the old priest back home says that gods once existed and there are no gods now because none believe in them. How could we after what happened to us? And how do I explain this to a madman?

Suddenly I feel sorry for Io. I wonder what his story is, who he has lost to end up here.

He's still looking out over the desert when his voice filters back to me. 'A sea of sand stretches where once there was water. There is an ocean here, but it's not mine.' He turns back to me. His eyes have paled to silver disks in the fickle light. 'I need you to take me back, back to the real ocean.'

My heart skips a beat and I almost drop the spoon into the stew. I see his lips tighten at the look on my face. 'The cities are all by the ocean,' I say. 'I can't take you there, it isn't safe.'

'Safe?' asks Io. 'What is there to fear?'

I hesitate. There's only one way to explain, and that's to show him, but I feel sick at the thought of exposing it. Still, I reach up and tug off my hat. I see his eyes widen as he takes in the line of ragged scar that crawls horizontally across my forehead: the telltale scar.

'This is why,' I say. 'In the cities, they capture you, slice out your brain and replace it with a mechanical one.'

Io gets to his feet. His face is unreadable. He stalks past the fire and kneels in front of me. He reaches for me, for my scar. I feel compelled to let him touch it. I barely feel his fingers as they trace the line of knotted skin.

His voice is hard. 'Who are "they"?'

'The wardens,' I reply. 'Dimensional travellers who overthrew humanity.'

'And these wardens, did they do this to you, child?'

I shrug, the pain of my past still stings, but I have learnt to bear it. 'I was lucky. They only managed to cut me before I escaped.'

His gaze drops and locks onto mine. The ghost of a sad smile curls the corner of his lip and suddenly he doesn't seem so wild or broken. 'And now here you are, remaining both strong and as beautiful as the tide.'

Io seems to come to some decision. He drops his hand, rises and moves to take his place back on the opposite side of the fire. His storm-like energy settles, and once again he begins to fidget with his hair. 'Take me to the ocean. I will ensure your safety, and much more.'

I'm not exactly sure why I agree to his request. Maybe I see something in his eyes that makes me feel as if I owe this to him, a complete stranger. Maybe I'm the crazy one, but the feeling is strong, compelling. So I'll be taking him to the ocean. Got to head back to town first for supplies, but nonetheless, I'm going.

The thought makes me feel nauseas. I can't believe I'm heading back—back to the city history once called Adelaide, but which is now known as Morte City. City of the Dead. I barely escaped last time.

While I can't see this ending well, Io oddly inspires me to have faith in him, faith enough for me to risk my life.

* * *

Io is sitting behind me on Cleopatra's back. His long-fingered hands rest lightly on my hips. Through the fabric of my shirt, I can feel callouses on his palms. I wonder what work a man does to get such hard hands. But Io's riding rhythm is smooth; it matches Cleopatra's gait with an easy rolling motion. Confident that he won't fall, I ease Cleopatra into a canter. She surges ahead, the salt-crusted Eyre Lake sand blooming in her wake.

The desert is a barren, flat stretch of land for the most part. Yellow and red-stained sand heaves and rolls across the flats, tossed by the errant forces of unrestrained winds. Saltbush, low and hardy, dots the expanse. The clusters of dusky green leaves and wizened branches are the only visual break between us and the horizon, and are all that lend perspective to the open space.

I take a deep breath. It's wild and lonely here, just like Io said—a dry ocean of sorts. But if you know where to look, there's more to find. There's shelter from the elements. Places to secure safety. Places like Sempre Town, one of the last hopes and homes of humanity.

* * *

It's almost dusk when we arrive. The sky arching over us is a bruised purple and pink, yet the last of the sun's rays puddle on the horizon, the colour a vicious red. I pull Cleopatra from her canter. The day's ride has not been easy on her, the weight of two people more than she's used to. She eases gratefully into a plodding walk.

A low ridge of rock rises up out of the sand ahead, the gate to Sempre Town cleverly concealed within its dark folds. I whistle to alert the sentry on guard. Cleopatra's ears flick forward as a low whistle is returned.

I glance back at Io. 'We'll rest here tonight and head out in the morning.'

Io nods, his eyes seeming to glow in the fading light.

The gate looks like a fall of saltbush growing tumbled against the weathered rock. It swings aside on mechanical arms as we approach, revealing a crevice wide and tall enough to let a horse and rider pass. I don't need to nudge Cleopatra through; she's happy to be home and eagerly noses her way into the stone corridor. Darkness falls as the saltbush gate settles back into place behind us.

The sound of Cleopatra's hooves clattering against the stone is almost deafening in the small space. But soon the corridor widens and the bright electric lights of Sempre Town assault our senses.

But the lights are all that's familiar. The sounds of human industry that usually fill the cavern are absent. There is a smell …

Io tenses at my back. Cleopatra snorts the stink from her nose and it takes all my effort to force her still. She wants to bolt and I can't blame her. But I need to find out what has happened.

'There is death here.' Io's voice is quiet, as if he fears to raise ghosts.

'Wait here with Cleopatra. I'll be back.' I slide out of the saddle, letting my boots ease gently to the ground. Io slides forward into the saddle. I feel exposed in the glare of the lights overhead, the cluster of small white eyes gathered together to look like an electric sun. I take a last glance at Io. On his nod, I head off.

The doors to the small stone dwellings ringing the main concourse all stand open. Usually these doors would house people, sitting at the thresholds peeling vegetables or filtering water through cleanser units. Their absence makes me uneasy. I get the distinct sense that this is no longer home; it feels more like I'm invading a tomb.

The first sign of foul play is a dark smudge of blood on a doorpost. Then I see the scorch marks along the buildings walls. My stomach drops and my heartbeat quickens; only one weapon I know of can make such marks—scar-bearer lightning guns.

I walk past several other scorched huts, slowly, quietly. The main concourse is just ahead. I clear the last building and find my friends. The scar-bearers didn't even bother harvesting them. I guess fifty humans didn't mean much to them in the scheme of things.

The people had been herded onto the concourse like cattle. I doubt they would have fought since half were mad and the others too fearful to pick up a weapon. But now their half-scorched, bloodied bodies lie tumbled in the centre of the open space. Their end was neither swift nor clean. Lightning guns brought to bear against you is a savage way to die.

I choke back my anger and my tears as I try not to take in the minute details of the slaughter.

I wish I could make them pay, the scar-bearers. But I'm only one person. I don't have the capacity for meaningful revenge any more than I have the time to grieve the loss. The scar-bearers could still be around.

A thought flashes into my mind: the whistle of the sentry at the gate. I feel like I'm choking on my stupidity. I turn to flee.

It's too late. A contingent of scar-bearers is already at my back.

Usually my scar is enough to deter idle interest in my identity, but this close they can't fail to see what I am. My eyes are green, not the copper orbs given to scar-bearers.

'Get her.' The leader's voice sounds mechanical. The flat tones fall from the once-woman's mouth like stones.

I turn. I run.

I leap forward onto the concourse. The stench of charred flesh is stronger here. I hold my breath as I leap over the tangled corpses. But the scar-bearers are fast. I hear the sizzle of their guns and I panic. I'm caught between now and my past. Back then I was running from other scar-bearers, blood sheeting down my face and the sound of lightning crackling at my heels.

I swallow the memories and redouble my efforts.

This time, there are no clinical white walls of an institute to navigate. This time, my way is clear. This time, there is rough stone and an exit known.

The lash of lightning comes out of nowhere. I stumble and fall, my arm screaming in pain. Just metres away, the scar-bearers advance. I am a dead woman. All I can do is close my eyes and think of the ocean from my dreams.

Suddenly I hear the screaming neigh of a horse. Cleopatra, mane flying and dark hooves flailing, emerges from the buildings. Atop her rides Io, dreadlocks snapping like whipped snakes around his angular face. He cries out a word in a language I don't understand. He holds his hand out to the side like a weapon, fingers stretched wide, and then water floods out of it in a torrent.

The scar-bearers fall like leaves before the onslaught. I see their legs and arms tossed within the maelstrom like trees in a storm. I hear their cries, and then hear them fade as they are washed away.

I push myself up to my knees, tasting salt as a wave crashes against my side and sprays into my face. I feel a strong hand grip the back of my shirt. Then I'm on Cleopatra's back behind Io, with the electric brightness of Sempre Town dwindling behind me. We're out under the clear sky again. A cool, night breeze flutters at my fringe.

'Are you all right?' Io sounds concerned.

'Yes,' I manage to say between breaths. 'Thanks to you.'

I place my forehead against Io's back and let him carry me away.

* * *

I'm dreaming. I am not sure why I always dream of the sea. Perhaps because it was the kindness of the sea and her fierce storms that hid me from prying eyes last time I escaped Morte City.

My dream is always the same. There is the ocean, an unnaturally blue stretch of water that matches the colour of Io's eyes. A man stands with his back to me at the tideline. He is a flat, black silhouette without detail, but I sense a storm of energy crackling around him.

'Will you come?' I ask him.

'Only if you remember,' he replies.

Then the ocean bursts into flames and they swallow the man.

I awake with a start. My fingers immediately reach for my whip. I find it coiled by my side, safe and sound. The smooth plaited leather beneath my fingertips feels like an old friend. I sigh. Then I remember Io with water streaming from his fingers. Was it a dream? It must have been, but I can't be certain.

It's morning and I'm surrounded by dense bushland. Overhead the sky glitters sapphire, but my view of it is fractured by a patterned lacework of branches and leaves. I sit up. A blanket falls off my chest. I recognise it as Cleopatra's saddle blanket. How did that get there? I have a vague recollection of being cold, and buffeted by wild winds and rain. Was I inside a storm? I can make no sense of what I remember; the images are disparate.

I look around. Cleopatra is grazing on green grass a few metres away. She snorts softly, the buckles on her loose reins gently chiming as she does.

Io, though, is nowhere to be seen.

I look around for him. Nothing. The tumble of trees and undergrowth extends for as far as I can see. Shades of green, brown and the occasional cascading cluster of yellow wattle blooms. It's been a long time since I saw anything but sand and saltbush. I can't deny the beauty in the landscape, but such beauty is dangerous.

The vegetation means I'm no longer in the desert. I'm close to the coast. And the coast means death.

The snap of a broken twig has me on my feet in an instant. Io steps out from behind a tree, his arms full of firewood. He looks different. He's dressed in a faded blue shirt and jeans slightly too short for him.

'Where did you get the clothes?' I ask.

Io drops the pile of timber next to me. 'I found an abandoned house back there.' He gestures over his shoulder. 'The clothes were inside.'

'Find anything else useful?'

A shadow clouds his eyes. 'Nothing worth noting.'

I haven't missed the specks of blood on the sleeve of his shirt, but choose to ignore them. 'Where are we?'

Io tips his chin to the ridgeline. 'Morte City is a league beyond that ridgeline. The ocean not much further than that.'

A league away? 'We were seven hundred kilometres away from here last night. How did we get here?'

Io kneels down and starts arranging small twigs into the beginnings of a fire. 'I carried us here. Your dreams gave me the strength to do it.' He lifts his gaze to mine, looking out from beneath his impossibly white eyebrows. 'Just as those same dreams had the strength to awaken me in the desert, so far away from the sea.'

Fragments of my dream suddenly surface in my mind: the blue ocean, the man, the fire ... 'What are you talking about?'

Io looks desperate. He leaves the fire and comes to sit beside me. He gathers my hands in the circle of his rough palms. 'Do you remember nothing of the past?'

I remember everything about my past: the blood, the pain and the fear. And I don't feel in the least like talking about it. 'What part of it exactly?'

Io grows still. 'The part when you were a warrior, when you formed deserts with your breath, when you protected the ancient pharaohs of Egypt.'

What the hell? Suddenly I feel stupid for having agreed to come here with him. He is beyond mad.

'I'm just as sane as you,' he says, reflecting my thoughts. 'More so, in fact, because at least I know exactly who I am.'

'And who is that?'

Io smiles a sad smile. 'The only other deity besides you on this planet.'

'Deity?'

'Yes,' says Io. 'The humans once called me Aegaeon, but I prefer to be known as Io.'

Aegaeon? I've read the histories: Aegaeon, the ancient Greek god of violent sea storms. Yeah, right.

'And who am I supposed to be, then?'

'You really don't remember anything, do you?' I hate how Io sounds as if he feels sorry for me. 'My dear, you are Sekhmet, Egyptian goddess of fire and healing.'

I choke back a snort of laughter. 'An Egyptian goddess, you say? And what would a Greek god and an Egyptian goddess be doing in the middle of Australia?'

Io shrugs. 'Maybe we're here to save the world.'

According to Io, I, apparently the goddess Sekhmet, was overthrown close to the end of the Egyptian dynasty. Cast out by my father Ra for defending a matter of justice, choosing the goddess Ma'at over him. My mind was wiped, he says, which is why I remember nothing.

It all sounds like a pile of crazy to me. But then again, the world is crazy. And there are the dreams I keep having.

'Stop calling me Sekhmet,' I say. 'My name is Sasha.'

Io sighs impatiently. 'It's fine if you won't accept who you are, but at least focus on the plan.' He's kneeling on the ground, stick in hand and drawing a map in the dust. 'Like I was saying, we'll wait out the daylight hours here, then travel on at dark.' He taps the stick in the dust, pointing to the ridgeline we will cross. 'If we can get me to the water, my powers will be restored.'

'Your powers?'

'Yes. Powers.'

I refrain from rolling my eyes. 'Then what?'

Io drops the stick. He looks surprised. 'We seek revenge. It's about time for it, don't you think? Time to avenge your friends that died in Sempre Town? Time to make the wardens pay for destroying the humans whose faith gave us life? We will fight. And we will win back Earth.'

He is caught up in these delusions of gods and men. Yes, I've lost friends, but what use is revenge? It only leads to more death. But Io looks determined, and I don't have the heart to cool his fervour.

He sits staring at me, waiting for my answer, waiting for me to rise with self-righteous indignation, waiting for me to wage war with him. But I can't do it. I've seen too much blood for one lifetime.

'Io, I—'

But Io is no longer looking at me. 'Shhh ...' He holds a finger to his lips. 'I heard something.'

The bush erupts.

Through a curtain of shredded tree bark and torn leaves, they burst ... the scar-bearers, ten of them.

As they run, the shifting sunlight shudders across the crumpled white scars marring each forehead. The scar-bearers' movements are fluid, unnatural, and their metallic eyes blaze with a hunger for battle and bloodshed. There is no humanity behind those windows to the soul, only a mechanical desire to destroy.

I'm on my feet in an instant. My whip is free, held loosely in my hand. I flick my wrist in a well-practised move, and the length of plaited leather ripples like the back of a snake. All thoughts of gods and men have fled.

Shit just got real.

The scar-bearers stop, fanned out around us. Their heavy navy-blue uniforms are pristine. Sharp-edged collars, perfect creases in the sleeves—the kind of perfection only a machine can achieve. I'm reminded of the warden's words I heard during my incarceration in Morte City: *Humanity is a flaw, with the brains of steel you are being gifted; you will become a race of perfection.*

But I look at the scars that mark the foreheads of the ten once-humans that stand before me. There is nothing of perfection in the ragged edged lines, only a reminder of individuality lost. Of gender lost. Beauty lost. Free will lost.

I'd rather die than exist like that.

'Ready to dance, guys?' I ask the assembled scar-bearers. 'Because you ain't taking me without a fight.'

They all sneer at me in perfect unison. Lightning guns are raised, again in unison, the tips snapping and crackling with the explosive energy harnessed within.

Io, now standing by my side, flicks a look of apology my way. 'Must've missed one at the farmhouse,' he says ruefully.

'Hell of a mistake to make,' I reply, raising my whip.

Two scar-bearers are down before the others have time to blink. I split the skull of one with the whip, metal brain gleaming through the rent in his bone, and put the other down screaming, clutching at the gash across her chest. The next falls, crushed under Cleopatra's deadly hooves as she flees terrified into the bush.

The seven remaining scar-bearers surge forward, a wave of fury interlaced with whippet-fast tendrils of piercing white electricity. Io is still by my side, fighting. In his fist he holds a tree branch, heavy with the weight of rugged bark and sun-dried hardwood. Another scar-bearer goes down screaming beneath the weapon.

Six left. Too many for us to finish.

Two scar-bearers rush toward me. There's nothing I can do but step backwards as they make it past the range of my whip. I see a flash of light from the end of the left scar-bearer's gun, and before I know it I'm on the ground, jerking and screaming as lightning coils around my limbs and boils my blood.

But it doesn't last. Io appears. His face is twisted with rage, dreadful and chilling. His eyes look like two blue coals in his face. I feel as if I will die if their focus falls on me.

I don't die. Suddenly I'm free of the lightning gun's grip. I roll to one side and manage to pull myself up. My lungs feel as if they are burning, my skin feels like it's peeled back to my bones. And I can't see Io.

He is hidden under a writhing mass of half-flesh, half-mechanical bodies. I can hear his roar of rage, a sound that turns to a sickening cry of abject pain. Then I hear the sneer and cruel laughter of his captors. They step back and I see Io on the ground.

His hands are bound wickedly with a barbed, copper chain. His face is red with blood, a blistered wound disfigures his belly, and his blue eyes are dulled with pain.

The scar-bearers have marked his forehead in their image.

All I can think is that if Io really were a god, he would never have let them do it.

Io's gaze searches, finds and fixes on me. His face changes as if he knows what I'm thinking. His look of pain and anger turns to horror, to desperation. 'No, Sasha,' he cries. 'Don't lose faith in me. Do *not* give up.' His voice rises to a shriek. 'I came as you asked, and now you need to remember.'

The words from my dream hit me like a slap to the face. In slow motion, I'm watching the scar-bearers coming for me, seeing their steps raising dust from the torn ground, seeing their uniforms rumpled and bloodied.

But I … I am lost in my mind. I am seeing a sea on fire—*my* fire.

I am remembering a man standing with his back to me at the tideline, and suddenly I know it is …

'Aegaeon!' The word tears out of my throat like a plea for life and it carries power.

With my belief, Io finds the strength he needs to build his storm.

I feel as if I'm abruptly plunged from air into ice water. I'm thrown sideways in the onslaught of Io's torrent of wind and rain. I half roll, half slide across the water-slick ground. I'm pulled up against the pile of firewood. I hold my forearm over my eyes, watching through spread fingers the tornado that rages in front of me. It is fifty metres high and twisting viciously. It plucks at the fully-grown trees and lifts deadfall in its wake. Torn leaves cascade around me

136

in a green rain. But best of all, within its embrace rides the corpses of ten scar-bearers. They look like spiders stuck in their own webs.

Victory.

I look about for Io. He's standing to one side, fists raised. The remains of the copper chain dangle from his blood slick wrists. His face is rigid with the effort to maintain his storm. But I can see he's flagging, his strength leaving his damaged body.

'Sasha, please help,' he grinds out from behind gritted teeth.

I get to my feet. I brace myself against the wind and pelting rain and make my way to his side. I place a hand on his shoulder. 'Call me Sekhmet,' I say.

Then Io falls to the ground unconscious and the storm fades.

* * *

I found my power when I claimed my name: Sekhmet, goddess of fire and healing. And while I still don't feel like an Egyptian goddess, I do remember now once being one.

Right now I'm on a beach, blue water lapping a short distance away. The copper and silver spires of Morte City rise in the near distance. Io lies on the sand with his head resting on my knees. He is weak, the damage inflicted on him far beyond my half-remembered skills to heal. But at least I've brought him to his precious ocean. I carried him here in a chariot I built of fire.

Io's eyes open. His irises have faded to grey. 'You believe me now?'

I run my hand over his knotted hair as a mother would a child. I ignore the crusted blood and the cut on his forehead that has now clotted over. 'I do.'

He smiles, a ghost of his old one. 'Are we by the ocean?'

'Yes.'

'Can you carry me to the water?'

I squeeze back my tears. Even dying, he still asks for the sea. 'Of course.'

He is heavy, but I manage to lift him clear of the sand. I struggle down the soft beach and onto the hard-packed stretch left by the receding tide. But when I hit the water, the waves suck the sand out from beneath my boots. I stumble and fall to my knees.

Io sighs as he feels the water close over his skin. His smile widens. 'Thank you for dreaming me awake,' he says. 'It's been good to walk the earth again, to not be forgotten ...'

I don't get a chance to reply because suddenly Io is gone. As I hold him, his body melts away to become sea foam, sand and water. For an instant, I smell rain and then it, too, is gone. Tears, hot and salty, begin to leak down my cheeks. I get to my feet and run my hand over my eyes.

It can't end like this. I won't let it end like this.

Slowly I raise my hands and stretch out my fingers. I watch sparks of my fire skip between their tips. Then I lift my eyes and look toward Morte City. I see the sea storm that's brewing over the bright spires and recognise the energy that feeds it.

And then I'm smiling. No, this isn't the end. It's just the beginning.

Io was right. It is time for revenge.

The Last Stronghold

Laid out before me are the skulls of ten sons. *My sons.* Once, the blood of gods and kings ran through their veins, but now all that remains is bone and memory. And I am the keeper of both.

The skulls stare at me as I wait in my ruined hall. The eye sockets are empty, but I imagine I can still see the spark of life that once animated them. Ten sons. It is a terrible thing for a father to lose so many. I touch the brow of each skull. The cold impregnated in the bone seeps into my fingertips.

Diaprepes, Azaes, Mestor, Elasippus, Autochthon, Mneseus, Evaemon, Ampheres, Eumelus ... Atlas.

Atlas. He was my firstborn and the first king of Atlantis. A bold lad in his youth, he grew to become a king, both respected and feared by all nations of the ancient world. But the human sycophants he kept company with betrayed him. Jealous of his power, they rose against Atlas and slew him, the final blow struck by a human he had honoured and called friend.

I loved Atlas, and his loss affected me deeply. In my grief, I set the ocean to rage for a full season. I razed clean the coasts of continents; I swallowed the ships and armies that dared to cross my waters. I taught the humans to fear me in a new kind of way.

The humans tried to placate me. They prayed to me and sacrificed their animals, but I took no notice. Nothing could replace the son taken from me.

Then things unravelled further. Following the demise of Atlas, my other sons began to fall. One by one, death claimed them, in ways neither quiet nor easy. My sanity frayed. I blamed humans for my grief and questioned why they were allowed to continue existing at all. Such cruel, selfish beings; they cared nothing of greatness nor higher purpose. Why should they prosper when my sons lay dead and cold?

My brother, Zeus, fearing what I would do, called me before him. As our king, his word was law. I pleaded with him to let me have my revenge, to let me flood the world.

But Zeus disagreed with my views. He was soft when it came to humans. 'They have such potential,' he told me. 'Given the chance, they will do great things.'

I spoke my truth to him. 'Believing such a thing, brother, shows you to be both weak and foolish.'

Zeus's temper was a forge easily flared and my words brought the weight of his ire upon me.

'You shall be bound to Atlantis,' he said, 'and sit there with your sons until you can devise another option for the future of humanity.'

And since then I have remained here. This dead island, this dead city. Atlantis.

Millennia have passed, and time has mellowed my anger. My imposed solitude has given me the distance I need to find clarity. I am now ready to leave this place, ready to reconsider Zeus's point of view. I think I have succeeded. My view now is that perhaps humanity just needs to be taught. And so I have devised a way.

With my trident, I carefully shave shards of bone from my sons' yellowed skulls. I mix the bone with my own blood in a bowl carved of stone, which has been passed through fire and doused with seawater. I fashion a glass egg and inside it place the embryo of a child who will grow to be the Heart of the World. She will be a mother for the human race, a woman who can teach them to honour the gods and to value peace over bloodshed.

I hear footsteps on the bridge leading to my hall. Yes. A treasure seeker has found the deep crack in the cliffs on the mainland—the great southern continent, the place I chose to conceal the door that leads beneath the sea and here to Atlantis. I shift in my seat. Anticipation wars with my dread. Perhaps this human will be one worthy of the Heart of the World and will help me win my freedom from Zeus's curse.

I take a deep breath and test the currents of sea air. I scent perfume. It is a woman that approaches.

The treasure seeker is closer now. Her hand is on the door, her shadow falling across the threshold. She enters hesitantly, a manmade weapon held at the ready. I do not look at her. Let her first see what is spread before me—the skulls of my sons—so I can judge whether my loss moves her.

The woman stops. She seems hesitant to approach. I raise my head, seeing my image reflected in the pools of her eyes.

I am immortal, but I look old now; my hair is white, and my brow weathered and wrinkled.

I ask the question that proves her worth to me. 'Can you name the firstborn son?'

She is a slight thing, tough and wiry as if she has travelled the hard places of the world and lived to tell the tale. Her hair is red; her eyes blue like the ocean on a clear day. Hope rises in my chest.

The woman lowers the weapon in her hand and approaches. 'May I?' she says, pointing to the line of skulls.

I nod; impressed by her bravery. She reaches over and picks up a skull. I watch her stagger under the sudden weight of it, the bones of a demigod being heavier than that of a man. But her instincts are sharp. They have led her true.

She has chosen the skull of Atlas.

Her eyes start to move as visions from beyond the plane of normal sight are revealed to her. I know what it is she sees. It is Atlas upon his throne, resplendent in his blood-red robes, his raven hair crowned with a circlet of gold.

The woman's breathing becomes ragged and she places the skull back down.

I taste her fear. It is metallic. My hope fades. Only a blameless heart could bear saying the name without fear. I ask her again. 'Can you name the firstborn son?'

For a moment she does not speak. Finally she whispers, 'Atlas.'

I hear the blood pumping in her veins. The blackness in her soul is revealed to me. I sigh. This woman is not the one. Prying into her thoughts, I see images of a man, a husband. A husband named Conner. There is blood on his face; she is standing over his corpse. This woman is a murderer.

She looks at me, her eyes wide with fear. I feel the egg secured within my chest twitch. The child inside it begs for release, but she is too precious a treasure to be given to one not worthy. My decision is made.

I grasp my trident and call forth my spirits of justice and vengeance: the furies.

They detach from the ceiling with a piercing cry, their talons outstretched and gleaming. But the woman is brave; I will give her that. She does not scream. Instead she raises her weapon and spits fire from it at the circling spirits. Three shots, and one by one they fall to the ground, wings thrashing a rain of green blood across the surfaces of my hall.

I reel with shock. The loss of the furies is too much, the weight of their blood too heavy on my conscience. My fragile peace shatters. Ancient rage is reborn. I raise my trident again, and backed with the full force of my anger I send it crashing to the ground. The floor splits, the crack running deep into the heart of Atlantis.

The earth begins to tremble.

The woman falls to the ground.

I reach into my chest, to the place where my heart once resided. From there I pull forth the delicate egg. The Heart of the World lays cradled within it, eyes closed and cupid lips serene. In her I see the promise to humanity that will never be fulfilled. I see my chance at freedom delayed. But I know myself a fool to have placed my hope in the hands of men.

I hold the egg in my fist and squeeze. The delicate glass cracks and the fluid within leaks out around my fingers. The baby starts to gasp in the now empty egg. My daughter is dying, just like her brothers before her.

'The Heart of the World,' I say to the woman.

Her eyes widen in surprise. Perhaps she is thinking of the husband she murdered. No. I see she harbours no regret on that score. She is thinking only of herself; thinking only of escape. But it is too late.

Seawater begins to leak in from the crack in the floor. The foundations of Atlantis are broken, and before long my last stronghold will be consigned to the waves. The water will not bother me. I can sit in this hall beneath the waves. I have the patience to await another chance at freedom. I will endure.

I am Poseidon.

The Poetry of Fire

I wipe the back of my hand across my brow. It comes away smudged with sweat-soaked ash. Sweat and ash—there is plenty of both around today.

It's midday, but the sky is dark, a thick grey soup that hovers heavily overhead. I look out across the patchwork of paddocks that blanket our valley. Usually dotted with cattle, they now stand empty, the herd moved elsewhere for their safety. The land looks naked without the animals. But the flames will soon change that.

This bushfire is coming. It's so close that I can see the glow of the flames over the tops of the sagging trees lining the valley rim. It's not a matter of *if* our farm will burn; it's only a matter of *when*.

'Lily!' Dad's voice breaks my reverie.

I jump to attention, swivelling my gaze to find him. He's by the shed, half leaning out of Bessie's cabin. Bessie is our old Leyland tractor. With Dad at her wheel, she has been patrolling the fence lines, keeping the firebreaks clear. Her usual bright-blue paintwork is hidden beneath a shroud of gunmetal-grey ash. The water tank fitted to her rear carryall has not fared much better.

But Dad looks worse. He's tired. His eyes are rimmed red beneath the old hat that sits crooked on his head. Ash has settled in the creases of his face, making him look older than his fifty years. I frown. He's pushing himself too hard. But my father refuses to accept that he's not as young as he once was; he's a stubborn old mule.

'Lily,' he repeats, starting to sound annoyed.

'Sorry, Dad, what is it?'

'Get Bobby and go check the back paddocks. Come get me if the fire has jumped the breaks. I'll be on the northern fence.'

I nod. Dad swings himself back into Bessie's seat. I see him close his eyes for a moment and take a deep breath. My heart goes out to him, but I know better than to tell him to rest. I hear Bessie's engine rumble to life and watch Dad reverse her out of the yard.

I push myself off the fencepost I'm leaning against and head for the stable. The gravel crunches beneath my boots as I hasten up the path. I push open the stable doors, their red-and-white paintwork startling against the grey backdrop of the day. It's warm inside. The smell of lucerne hay and oiled leather rises to greet me.

I let my eyes adjust to the dimness. I see the horses shuffling in the rear pens. Only two remain; we've sent the others off with the cattle.

I smile as I reach up to pat their long noses. Bobby and Gentry. They could almost be twins. Matching palomino coats and the white blaze down each of their noses makes them almost indistinguishable from each other. But their eyes give it away. Bobby has more sass in him than Gentry.

Both animals stare at me as I reach up to get my saddle. Their wide brown eyes regard me with equine disapproval. I smile wider. For horses, these two have attitude. They know what they like, and a stinky, sweaty rider is not it.

I hang my saddle over my shoulder and move into Bobby's pen. He sidles away from me, but I grab his halter and pull him closer. He tries to bite me, but there's no heart in it, he just wants me to know that he isn't pleased about this. I push his nose away, slide the saddle onto his back and fit the bridle bit. He resolves to walk slowly as I open the gate and lead him out. Gentry nickers as we leave. He doesn't like to be left alone.

Bobby settles into a gentle trot as we head for the back paddocks. Smooth rolling land soon gives way to thick scrub, the undergrowth dotted here and there with the larger mottled trunks of spotted gums. The track is only a faint line between the trees, more suited to kangaroos than a large horse and rider. But nonetheless, I turn Bobby and head along it.

Around us the bush is unnaturally quiet. I remind myself that wild animals are smarter than humans. They would have left at the first scent of smoke. But I find that's not the case for all of them.

I almost jump out of my skin when a wallaby skitters out from beneath Bobby's feet. Bobby shies sideways as the animal, moving fast, almost falls over its own tail. The wallaby rights itself and bounds away. I watch it expertly navigate through the bush, strong hind legs kicking up deadfall and dust in its wake. I find myself hoping the fire doesn't catch it.

The back paddocks are made of rougher land than the smooth green spread closer to the homestead. Groves of wattle, gum and she-oak trees huddle close here. Their wild tangles of limbs are thick with dead leaves and hanging shreds of tattered bark— perfect fodder for a bushfire.

I smell the smoke before I see the flames, hear the poetry in the crackle and snap of burning timber. Bobby hesitates as I try to push him forward, but a kick to the ribs and he reluctantly follows my instruction. His barrel chest pushes through the undergrowth until the last thicket of wattle branches gives way to him.

The view opens out as we top a low ridge.

And in the passage of one moment we have passed from quiet bushland into hell.

The back paddocks are alight, and it's not with the quiet pop and crackle of a contained campfire. I hear the elated roar and boom of a full-blown summer bushfire.

Waves of intense heat buffet me. Sweat dries off my skin almost instantly. This inferno is raging. Nothing will stop it now.

I turn Bobby on his heel and he's only too happy to respond. I head for the northern fence. My heart is thumping, but I hold Bobby back from a full gallop. The ground is too rugged. We make good time. But I fear the fire is faster.

I see the first flames on my right: yellow-and-red shards of light crackling through the wattle tangle. Then they are on my left. The flames are flanking me. I choke back a sob and ignore the rolling white of Bobby's eye. I hold the reins close, holding him back from the flight he wishes to take.

But as I said, Bobby has sass. And sometimes he makes his own decisions.

Bobby shakes his head and tears the reins free from my grip. I try to grab at his mane as he careens down the track. My fingers slip. My thighs burn with the effort to hold on. But Bobby jumps across a fallen log …

I fall.

I am laid out flat on my back in the middle of the track. My ankle is screaming in pain and my wrist is no better. I struggle to sit upright. I look up the track. All that's left of Bobby is the slowly settling dust he has left in his wake.

'Goddammit!'

I try not to look at my ankle. The odd way it sits out to one side is enough to tell me that I won't be walking anywhere anytime soon. I hold my wrist to my chest; the grating of bone against bone makes my stomach turn. I sit for a moment and try to gather my thoughts. Around me, the bush is still silent except for the sound of the approaching fire.

Snap. Crack. Pop.

I huddle over my injuries, trying to sort my options. Bobby will head straight for home, but Dad won't be there to meet him. I need a plan, but the pain is making me dizzy. And the flames that have been flanking me have grown closer. I feel the heat of them; feel the oxygen being burnt out of the air around me.

Suddenly I know I'm going to die here. I rest my forehead on the knee of my good leg and try to focus on breathing.

I hear a noise. It's a sizzling sound, like when steak is put onto a hot barbeque. I look up. The fire is even closer now. It hugs the track, but in patches, not yet the wall of flames that marks a bushfire frontline.

Out of one of those patches, a solitary tower of flame emerges. Roughly three metres high, it walks on two legs like a human. Despite the heat, I feel a chill run up my spine.

I watch as it circles me. I try to sit up straighter, as if by doing so I can alleviate my fear. My ankle protests the movement and I almost faint. I stop moving, sucking in deep breaths of smoke-scented air to try and maintain consciousness.

The flame tower is humanoid in shape. Darker flames flicker where the eyes and mouth should be, paler flames mark wild licks of hair, fingers and a penis. The mouth of the creature opens and from it I hear words I can't understand. They are melodious in their strangeness.

'What do you want?' My voice falters.

The creature steps forward. He kneels by my foot. His fiery gaze takes in the awkward angle of my ankle. He looks back at me.

Injured? The word is a not quite a whisper, as fragile as smoke.

I feel some of my fear melt away. I look at him. 'Yes. My ankle and wrist.'

Gently, the fire sprite gathers up my broken wrist and ankle, one in each of his hands. I'm surprised to find I don't burn at his touch. Instead, it feels almost cool.

I watch my skin start to painlessly flake away. Beneath, my exposed muscles unravel to reveal my bones. The shattered shards appear like a tumbled jigsaw. The sprite lets go and starts to trace his fingertips across the broken edges. To my surprise, they begin to knit. But the fractures are not glued with new bone; they are held together by virtue of solid fire. Gleaming seams are left behind, the repairs feeling stronger than the clean bone ever did.

I look up at him. He smiles.

He removes his fingers. I watch my muscles regrow of their own accord, glowing strands of flame that twist up into my forearm and leg. Then skin, fashioned from gleaming sheets of red-gold fire, blooms to cover the wounds. I touch it. Beneath my fingertips, the new skin thrums with music. I can almost make out words impregnated in the sound; lines of poetry, full of emotion.

The light fades and soon my skin looks like normal skin again, but beneath it I can still feel the fire in my bones. The fire sprite stands up and holds out a hand to help me to my feet. I rise, testing the function of my wrist and ankle. There is no pain anywhere. I can make it home now if I run.

'Thank you,' I say to him.

He nods, his pale hair waving gently around his thin, angular face. But before he can do anything else, a rumbling noise fills the air, a sound I know well: the sound of a tractor.

Bessie.

Dad is coming.

The fire sprite's gaze snaps up to follow the line of the trail. I can see fear flickering in the dark flames of his eyes. He turns to run, but I grab him by the arm.

'It's okay. It's just my dad.'

The sprite shakes his head violently; he struggles, pulling his arm out of my hand. But it is too late.

Bessie rounds the corner and with her comes a rain of water. My father has the water tank nozzles open, jets of liquid spraying wide down each side of the track. Water overspray curls around us.

The fire sprite has nowhere to go. He stops and turns to look at me. I see the horror and resignation in his eyes.

'No!' I cry.

As the water touches him, his eyes thin to slits and the dark flame of his mouth opens into an O-shape. His cry is a long drawn-out note, both beautiful and heartbreaking in its purity. His breathing quickens. His skin begins to hiss, large areas of it darkening to patches of charcoal that spread across his chest and stain his pale hair grey.

His cry stops. The silence that follows is sickening.

His body crumbles, piece by piece, to the ground.

I barely notice my father jumping from Bessie's cab and running to grab me up in a relieved hug.

'Bobby found me. I'm so sorry, love. I'm so sorry ...' He keeps saying it over and over.

All I can think about is how sorrowful is the sound of flames being doused by water.

References

'Music Box Witch' first appeared in the anthology *Perspective*, Geelong Writers Inc, December 2016.

'I, Mutineer' (previously titled 'The Fate of Mutineers' first appeared in *AntipodeanSF* magazine, issue 226, May 2017.

'Spirit of the Earth' first appeared in the anthology *Flourish*, Morrison Mentoring, December 2015.

'Greysin's March' first appeared on the Katharine Susannah Prichard Writers Centre news blog, December 2016.

'Tattoo' first appeared in the CSFG/Conflux 12 convention handbook, September 2016.

'The Darkness has Teeth' first appeared in the anthology *Dead of Winter*, Mighty Quill Books, March 2017.

'Blue Moon' first appeared in the anthology *Nocturnal Natures*, Zimbell House Publishing, USA, September 2016.

'The Southern Cross' first appeared in the anthology *The Outback*, Boolarong Press, June 2016.

'This Wild Stretch of Ocean' first appeared in the anthology *Brio*, the Fellowship of Australian Writers, Queensland, November 2015.

'The Last Stronghold' first appeared in *The Lost Door: A Zimbell House Anthology*, Zimbell House Publishing, USA, August 2016.

About the Author

Pamela Jeffs is a prize-winning speculative-fiction author living in Queensland, Australia with her husband and two daughters. Her work has been published previously in various magazines and anthologies, both nationally and internationally.

Prior to pursuing her passion for writing, Pamela's background was in interior and exhibition design. This allowed her to collaborate with a multitude of talented artists and designers across a number of artistic platforms.

Red Hour and Other Strange Tales is her debut collection, and features both new and previously published award-winning work.

To discover more books by Pamela Jeffs and be notified of new releases, deals and specials, visit and subscribe at:

www.pamelajeffs.com
Twitter: @Pamela_Jeffs
Facebook: @pamelajeffsauthor